Damon,
My brother life
we get to rewri
I wouldn't era:
You've inspired me more than you'll ever
know, I can't wait to see what the
future has in store. God Bless you!!

The Compass of a Conscience

BY

Darnell D Wright

Note:

Unauthorized sale of this book is deemed illegal under the United States Copyright Laws. Printing and selling of this book without the publisher's authorization may be deemed illegal and punishable under the law.

Although based in part on actual events that occurred in the author's life, this is a work of fiction. Any resemblance to real people, living or dead, actual events, establishments, organizations, and/or locales are intended to give it a sense of reality and authenticity. Other names, characters, places and incidents are either products of the author's imagination or are used fictitiously, as are those fictionalized events and incidents that involve real persons and did not occur or are set in the future.

Published by: DWRIGHTBOOKS PUBLISHING 10411 South Drive #819 Houston, Texas 77099 www.dwrightbooks.com

ISBN: 9781973347859 Library of Congress Copyright 1-5626897111 Cover: JoshuaJadon.com Design: EverythingByDesign Interior Layout: JoshuaJadon.com Website Design: justmarshall.com All rights reserved, including the right to reproduce this book or portions thereof in any form whatsoever. *DWRIGHTBOOKS PUBLISHING* © 2017

Published by: DWRIGHTBOOKS PUBLISHING LLC

Foreword

by

Kam Ellis, M.Ed
Author and educator

Booker T. Washington said, "Success is to be measured not so much by the position that one has reached in life as by the obstacles which he has overcome." This quote is telling in the life of my dear friend and colleague, Darnell Wright. His tireless dedication to this book, *The Compass of a Compass* is remarkable, as I look back on our countless conversations and his late nights of writing in order to properly convey his story to readers. As an avid reader of literary biographies, I gravitate to the stories of individuals that possess the grit and tenacity to press through the hardships faced in life. *The Compass of a Compass* is a story of hardship and redemption. Darnell used his experiences of life on the hard streets of Pensacola, Florida and his incarceration to touch the lives of wayward youth by building relationships that undoubtedly related to their individual struggles. The events of his life such as growing up in poverty, the lessons taught by his unschooled, but wise grandmother, and the death of his brother take readers on a journey of the rawness of his reality, road to self-discovery and hope. *The Compass of a Conscience* chronicles Darnell's mentorship of Brandon, and how that relationship awakened true purpose in him that he wasn't aware of was there. The Compass of a Conscience tackles the depths and complexity of life that many are sheltered from. It is my hope that many read this book and see the humanity of the experiences, and how we are not all afforded with the same opportunities. With this consciousness, we should not be swift to judge another without knowing their full story. I also hope that others use the book as evidence that you can rise above circumstances brought on by meager beginnings, or even by your past mistakes. Credibility cannot be distorted when it is based upon not only experience, but awareness and the willingness to reflect upon oneself. Mr. Wright has done this inner work, and *The Compass of a Conscience* was birthed because of it.

"If you want to lift yourself up, lift up someone else."

- Booker T. Washington

Forward

By

Dennis Ketler Larry

I met Darnell Wright seven years ago. A federal judge in the Northern District of Florida asked me to help, to mentor Darnell. He had recently been released from federal prison in Atlanta, where he served several years for a major drug trafficking conviction. Before prison he had made a very lucrative living in the drug trade. Now he was being returned to society to make his way, to make an honest living, and to resist the pressures from others in his old neighborhood to return to his former life. The adjustment to this new life would be as tough a thing as he had done in his life. Getting and holding employment now presented a high probability of failure. And how easy it would be to be tempted to return to the drug trade.

Would I help this man? Of course. I would try. I felt ill equipped to be his mentor. Why would he even consider listening to any advice I might offer? Would we like each other? Would we respect each other's points of view? Would the mentor-mentee relationship survive for long?

Seven years later Darnell is working hard, running a business. He is successful in his business, but it came with sacrifice. He had tried to get in the concrete business, but couldn't get the work from general contractors he would need to succeed. But with hard work and a lot of risk, and determination to earn well and earn honestly, he now owns his own company, and is happy, and provides for his family.

Through this process of Darnell's re-entering society, our relationship has remained close. We took meals together. He shared is faith in Christ and gave me books to read that influenced his faith. He invited me to attend, and even participate in, volunteer group therapy sessions in which he engaged with very troubled youths serving in a detention center. I watched him turn his very tough life experiences into lessons that seemingly got through to troubled teens who couldn't be reached by other adults. He became their coach, if you will, by telling them the brutal truths about where bad life decisions lead. He became their mentor.

And oddly, he became my mentor in an unexpected juxtaposition of roles. His faith in Christ helped make my faith stronger. His amazing optimism that his struggles would enable him to succeed in an almost impossible endeavor to overcome his situation as an ex-convict inspired me more than any inspiration I ever offered him.

Darnell's book, Compass of Conscience, tells the story of his life. He believes deeply that his story can be of help to others. And it can be. This is a book anyone can benefit from reading, but particularly it can benefit young men and women who can use a little guidance to get their lives straight. And on top of everything, his story is one which readers like me have hardly ever realized is one lived by a lot of our society.

Dennis Ketler Larry is a trial attorney who practiced law for forty years in Pensacola, Florida before retiring. He lives in Atlanta with his wife Barbara, and enjoys spending time with his daughter and her family. He has a son in New York and three fine young grandsons.

DEDICATIONS

I'd like to dedicate this book to Christ Jesus my savior first. Next to my mother Wanda Wright (On next page) for her valuable upbringing and to all the wonderful women in my life whom I have the privilege to call mom. **Priscilla Moore, Linda Porter, Geraldine Wells, Teri Lynn Dunn, Brenda Steans-RIH.**

To all who are still living... Annie Steans, Rutha (Willie) Hardaway, Lonnie May Savage, Lula Devaughn, Jennifer Jones Butler, Lillie James, Cynthia Gipson, Frances Marks Moore, Rhonda (Donald) Rice, Dematriss Boyd, Rivers

(Candy) Hesters, Mary May, Francine Williams, Ola Mae Johnson, Gwen (Micheal) Johnson, and Kym Tucker Lewis Davis. The Wisdom, Knowledge, and Love I get from all of you is the reason I'm able to enjoy the quality of life that I take pleasure in living today. You have made me feel like the luckiest man alive to have your love and support. I love you all.

Sending love to my family at:

Pentecostal Temple (The church that raised me.) Bishop John D Young Sr.- Pensacola, Florida

Friendship Missionary Baptist (The church that made me.) Rev. LuTimothy May- Pensacola, Florida

I send my sincerest love to all my family, friends, and most of all, to the young boys and girls who are struggling to find themselves and their purpose in life. Please read and enjoy!

FAMILY AND FRIENDS

Raised in an area known as "A Street," I know some of the greatest people on earth. I would love to name everyone individually, but I simply can't because I do not want to forget anyone. Just know you all mean the world to me.

Much love to:

Mythiquer Pickett- I love what you're accomplishing with "WE SEE ABILITIES"...

To all of the *Fallen One's*, who tragically lost their lives to the streets and to those who are still incarcerated... I say to you, God is still in control!

A special salute to:

My hometown of Pensacola, Fl. and the many sections thereof- The entire Westside and Eastside of Pensacola, The Avenues, Pensacola Village, Warrington, Tan Yard, Aragon Court, Attucks Court, Gonzalez Court, Moreno Court, Morris and Sanchez courts, Garnett Circle, Escambia Arms, Truman Arms, Shanny Town, Cow Town, Montclair, Mayfair, Erress, Wedgewood, Brent, Brownsville, Bells Head, Bellview, Myrtle Grove, Ensley, Lincoln Park, Cantonment, Century, Molino, Milton, Barth, Pace, Gulf Breeze, Navarre, Perdido Key...

Did I miss anybody? I hope not.

Although I have moved on, I could never forget where I came from. I just want to say, Thanks!

ACKNOWLEDGEMENTS

The journey of this book has been somewhat of a hand to hand ordeal. From its inception and throughout the entire process, there have been several people that I would dare not be negligent in giving honorable mention to.

Douglas Allen

It was you that planted the seed that inspired me to write about my life. I can still hear you quoting "Darnell, there's a book in you," fresh in my mind today as vividly as I did years ago when you said it to me for the first time. You saw down the corridors of time and predicted this book. What a person you are, what a gift you have, and I thank you.

M Casey Rodgers

Life has this unscripted way of bringing people who seem to be the most improbable together. That statement couldn't have been more conclusive than that of our story. It is one that should and very well could become a book in of itself one day. What you've done for me and countless of others with the Re-entry program is nothing less than stellar. I can't begin to give enough thanks to you and all the volunteers of the Re-Entry program and its investors (Dr. Zieman and Renfroe-Thank you both for giving me an amazing smile.) for improving the quality of so many lives. There's only one individual I know like you and that person is you. I thank you for believing in me and taking a risk on me.

Dennis Larry

My dear friend I wrestle to find the words befitting someone with a character as gigantic as yours. You and your lovely wife Barbara welcomed an ex-convict into your home and treated me like I was family. You've been a mentor and as faithful of a friend as it gets, and for that I pay the utmost homage to you. Your edits of the original manuscript and your edits of the current version of this book has lain a solid foundation for me. This is a small token of my gratitude to you. I thank you for your contributions to this book and my life.

Kameetra Ellis

Meeting you Ms. Ellis is one the greatest events of my life. What you've been and mean to me is inexpressible. Whenever I tried to slow down you sped up and you never ceased to remind me of who I am when I seem to have forgotten my purpose and mission. You are a true friend indeed, but I call you special because it is the best description of how rare a gem you are. Your contributions to this book and my life is greatly appreciated.

Pheadra Liddell

Writing heartfelt words to you is second nature to me. In every area of my life, you've been there. In moments of despair you were there, in times of need you've taken what you had and didn't hesitate to share, even to this day you continue to care. Not many have held me down like you have and I thank you from the bottom of my heart for your contributions to my life and to this book.

Eunicia Giuchici

I'm cognizant of the fact that you don't like to be honored for things you do from the heart, but it would be a terrible disservice on my behalf if I didn't honor you. The person you are I could only aspire to be. Your help and advice have always been on point whenever I needed it. You truly are one of a kind. It was you who saw something special in me that day in the courtroom and it's only right that you and "The Boys Base" are the inspiration for this book. I thank for your contributions to my life and to this book.

To every organization who have entrusted the youths in their care to me: The Pensacola Boys Base; Oliver Jones- Words cannot express how grateful I am that you trusted me the way you did with your organization. What's up William Freeman? Good dude and outstanding leader. Also, a warm thank you goes out to Julie Adams. You're the nicest person I've ever met.

To the Goodwill Easter Seals/AMIKids- Jeronda Jerralds Golston your tireless work and dedicated to the youths of Escambia County is remarkable. You should be honored. I dare not forget The Henry and Rilla White Foundation, Teen Court and most of all... the lives of each teen that was touched being mentored by me. This book is in commemoration of you.

TABLE OF CONTENTS

Chapter 1 The Big Break 1

Chapter 2 The Tender Years 8

Chapter 3 History Lesson 12

Chapter 4 One in the Same 16

Chapter 5 Special Delivery 20

Chapter 6 Disaster Strikes 26

Chapter 7 Guilty Conscience 35

Chapter 8 Recess 38

Chapter 9 What A Lady 41

Chapter 10 Cut from a different Cloth 48

Chapter 11 Freedom 52

Chapter 12 The Offer 55

Chapter 13 A Fresh Start 58

Chapter 14 The Riot 66

Chapter 15 Power Struggle 69

Chapter 16 Eyes Wide Open 74

Chapter 17 Uninvited Guest.................83
Chapter 18 Date with Destiny.............86
Chapter 19 Checking in......................96
Chapter 20 Memory Lane...................99
Chapter 21 Moving Too Fast.............104
Chapter 22 Heart to Heart.................109
Chapter 23 Misplaced Anger.............115
Chapter 24 The Robbery...................120
Chapter 25 Time to Go.....................125
Chapter 26 The Good News..............135
Chapter 27 It's A Miracle..................138
Chapter 28 The Proposal..................141
Chapter 29 Instant Karma.................144
Chapter 30 Lies, Deceit, and Betrayal............147
Chapter 31 History Repeats Itself...................155

Chapter 1
The Big Break

May 4th, 2011 was probably just another typical day to most people, but not to a guy named Donnell White. To him, there was nothing typical about that day at all. That day would become what he'd often refer to as his *second chance at life*, the moment when he knew his life would never be the same again.

At the Holcomb County Jail, located in Holcomb, Fl., a young man is sitting inside of a 6 ft x 10 ft two bunk cell. The young man is being held at this location because it has a contract with the government to act as a hub for housing federal inmates. Dressed in an orange jumpsuit, he's waiting to be transported to a Federal Courthouse in Pensacola Fl., where his case, overturned on a successful appeal, will be resentenced.

He's already served three years of the 15-year sentence currently imposed on him. His "celly," the person whom he shares the cell with, is sound asleep. For this young man though, sleeping is the farthest thing from his mind. Anxiously, he paces the short distance from the cell bars to the small rectangular window at the back of the cell he's in. The scheduled time for his court appearance is 9:15am.

His eyes are now fixated on the circular clock that hangs on the wall in the common area outside of his cell. It is now 8:40am, and he wonders why the officers haven't come to get him yet. His patience starts to wear thin and just as he wraps his hands around the bars to squeeze them, a voice comes across the intercom.

"White..."

"Yeah!" He replies.

"You got court this morning. Come on out."

He releases the bars and backs up to wait for the door to unlock. A loud buzzer sounds, and a distinctive click follows. He slides the door from right to left and exits his cell into the common area to wait for the arrival of the officers assigned to escort him. Familiar with jailhouse protocol, he stands in a designated red square box painted on the floor in front of the door.

Two officers are standing on the other side of the door with handcuffs, shackles, and ankle cuffs. The door unlocks and there, immediately on the floor where the officers stand, is another painted red square box. One officer orders him to turn around, place his hands on the door and spread his legs. He tells him to lift one leg at a time as he puts the ankle cuffs on him, and again to turn around so that he can put the shackles and handcuffs both around his waist and wrists.

Then the two officers escort him, one in the front and the other behind him, down a long hallway. By the time they reach the end of the hallway one of his escorts radios in, "Run Central" and the door immediately slides open. The first officer enters and takes him to a long desk where he notices a file with his name on it, last name first and first name last, in bold black lettering.

The officer grabs the file and they lead the young man to the Sally Port. The Sally Port is an area of the jail where prisoners are secretly brought in and transported out of an institution. The officers then place him in the backseat of a cruiser heading to the United States District Courthouse in Pensacola, Fl.

The ride for this guy isn't comfortable but it is an intense one indeed. Thoughts racing through his mind at a pace beyond his control, he can't help but to think about the potential outcome of his situation. He's had success getting to this pivotal point, but he just can't seem to shake the fear that something could easily go sour for him. As quickly as his confidence began to build, he fears facing the same federal prosecutor and sentencing judge he faced a few years prior, and a cloud of gloom casts over any positive expectations he tries to have.

They arrive soon to the south gate of the courthouse where they are met by outer perimeter security. On the other side of the gate, a guard shack is within eye view of the vehicle. A guard exits the shack, approaches the vehicle, and asks the transporter for the appropriate paperwork for the inmate they're bringing in. Once the paperwork is verified, a signal is given to the guard inside the control room of the guard shack. The gate opens, and they proceed inward to the heavily guarded Sally Port of the courthouse.

Once inside, a large metal gate comes down and secures the entire area. The officers exit the vehicle and escort their prisoner to a special entrance at the back of the courthouse. After being buzzed through several doors the inmate finally arrives at a holding cell.

He sits down on a bench made from solid concrete as his eyes scan every inch of the cell. Noticeably etched on the walls of the holding cell that he's in are writings and quotes left behind by previous felons. Name dropping the names of inmates who snitched, and vulgarities are expressed in various ways. One sentence that catches his immediate attention reads:

"So and So was here on this day and was sentenced to LIFE!!"

"LIFE REALLY SUCKS."

Donnell will remain in this cell until he's summoned for his court appearance. In what has become some sort of a ritual for him, he stands up, turns around and kneels to pray. "Dear Heavenly Father, it is in your Holy Son's name Jesus

Christ that I pray. I confess my sins and ask for your mercy as I stand condemned by the world. I know that you are greater than the world—"

As he is praying, the buzzer echoes and he hears someone with a set of keys approaching. Two US Marshalls walk into the cell to frisk him for any illegal contraband he might have smuggled in. Then he is taken to an elevator and is escorted into a courtroom on the 5th floor. As he enters the room, he is surprised and a bit perplexed to find himself inside a packed courtroom full of strangers. He notices his family seated on the opposite side of the courtroom. The Marshalls lead him to a table where his attorney is seated, smiling. The Marshalls give him a brief tutorial of court procedures. Then, he's instructed to take a seat next to his attorney, and he exchanges a handshake with him. The two of them lean toward each other for a private conversation.

His attorney whispers, "I know you're probably wondering who these people are and why they're all here. This is a group of teenage youth offenders from the Ohallowbee Detention Center for Boys. The other individuals are staff and parents of the boys—" The attorney is interrupted by the bailiff's announcement, and the voice of the court security officer fills the room.

"All Rise. The Honorable Stacy Ransom presiding. Maintain order in the court."

Judge Ransom enters, sits down and says, "You may be seated."

Donnell's attorney turns toward him and whispers again, "I'll fill you in later, O.K.?"

In a very formal and professional manner Judge Ransom states, "This is case number 45900CS. The United States versus Donnell White. This is quite an unusual occurrence for me. I don't normally have any criminal defendants that come back before me on *habeas corpus*. Quite frankly, it's extremely rare. It is also to my understanding that we have some special guests in attendance today from the Ohallowbee Detention Center for Boys. I sincerely hope you boys pay close attention to what you are about to witness today, and I hope that you realize that the path each of you are on could easily land one, if not all of you, right here in front of me. Perhaps even in the very same seat occupied by Mr. White here, facing the consequences of your actions.

With all that said I believe that we are ready to proceed with Mr. White's case. Is Mr. Cain present on behalf of the prosecutor's office?"

"Good morning, Your Honor. Tony Cain for the United States Attorney's Office."

"How about Mr. Gilliam on behalf of the Federal Public Defenders Office?"

"Yes, Your Honor. Durley Gilliam, appointed counsel for the defendant today."

"What I'd like to do today," Judge Ransom says then, "that is, if it's ok with both the counsel and Mr. White, is allow these boys to hear Mr. White talk about his life and about the experiences he's had living this kind of lifestyle, in his own words. I hope that you boys listen very carefully to the things Mr. White is about to share with you all today. You guys really need to take heed of any advice he can offer. It might someday be useful in helping you all avoid making the same mistakes that he himself has made. Mr. White, would you be interested in speaking to these young men today?"

"I would love to, Judge. It would be an honor for me to share my story and give them some insight. I believe that I might have knowledge that can relate to their situation and help them," Donnell replies.

"Very well then, you may turn and address them. On second thought, wait a minute Mr. White," Judge Ransom says. She beckons for one the Marshalls. "May I have his handcuffs removed? I want him to feel comfortable as he's telling his story."

"Thank you," Your Honor.

"You're welcome," Mr. White.

"Hello everybody. Since you have sat through the formalities of this hearing today it should be evident what my name is by now. I'll spare you guys the trouble of having me restate it to you. I believe that if I'm to tell you all a story what better one to tell than that of my own. You see, it's *my story*. Can't nobody tell my story better than I can because I'm the one that lived it.

Have you guys ever heard someone say of a cancer patient that passed away, he or she fought a long hard fight? Well, that's the kind of analogy about to be used here today about the outcome of my life thus far. The difference is that I didn't lose my life to the cancerous plague of violence, drugs, and prison. I lived through it all to give guys like yourselves and others my testimony.

I got to admit that I've always felt like I've been dying to live, but only living to die. Seriously. It is only by the grace of God that I'm alive and well to share my story here today. Do you all understand what I'm saying thus far?"

"Yeah. Uh huh," they respond simultaneously.

"You guys are getting a sneak peek into your future to see what's in store if you don't heed the warning being given to you today. I'll be the first one to tell you that this journey of mine has been troublesome, transforming, and spiritual."

Chapter 2
The Tender Years

"I jumped off the porch at the tender age of twelve years old. For those of you who have absolutely no clue of what that means, it is a euphemism, meaning that I graduated from my innocence to live a life of corruption. It felt like the ultimate transition from being a little boy to becoming a grown man, like some of you boys may be feeling right now.

I've been in juvie detention too and I know what it feels like to be sitting where you're sitting. This isn't my first rodeo, ya know? I know what it felt like thinking that I was a mature adult at times but couldn't quite control that little boy inside of me. Some of the adults, if not all, in this room have had a few of those same emotions when they were your age too. But unlike us, their choices didn't land them in any trouble like ours have.

I've sold drugs basically all my life and my history with drugs runs deep. I've never had a real father figure in my life, so I looked up to the closest males around me at that time. Those individuals so happen to be my uncles.

My uncles dealt drugs and were deep into the pimping scene as well. I had one uncle that I absolutely idolized and wanted to personify so badly. His name was Uncle Russell. Curtis Mayfield had a song out back then that was somewhat of an anthem in the streets called *Pusherman*. During that time, uncle Russell seemed to have been the epitome of that song. It blew my mind how he had the *Colors of the Rainbow* as he was known to call them.

One of his most infamous quotes that I recall hearing him say all the time was, "*I don't go anywhere where my rainbow isn't there. My rainbow always leads me to a pot of gold.*"

His *Colors of the Rainbow* were the women he pimped of diverse ethnicities and backgrounds. They were black, white, Mexican, and if my memory serves me well, there was an Asian woman among them too. He called each of them his girlfriend. I was blown away at how they all got along at the same time and place for the same person.

At the tender age of 10 years old, I had my first encounter with drugs and money. Another uncle of mine named Uncle Wimp had just been released from completing a 15-year prison sentence for drug related charges. Uncle Wimp shared the same criminal mindset as his brother Russell did.

The only difference between the two was that uncle Wimp was crazy as hell. Little did I know then that he'd be moving in with us. One day I came home from school to an empty house and I went straight to what use to be my bedroom. As I turned the knob and opened the door there it

The Compass of a Conscience

was, just staring at me. For a very poor kid who had never seen the likes of a fifty-dollar bill, there were literally hundreds of them lying on my bed.

I froze in amazement at first until I noticed two clear sandwich bags filled with squares that I considered to be brown pencil erasers.

Ok, let me explain to you guys why I thought they were erasers. Back then in school we had these thick, brown, square shaped erasers. To be able to visualize what I'm describing you'd have to be at least thirty years old to know anything about those kinds of erasers. Turns out, I had innocently mistaken the squares, which I later found out to be heroin, for the erasers we used in school.

"Are you guys getting it yet?"

Grabbing one from the bag, I began to use it on my homework. Strangely, it left a brown smear on my paper, so I stopped using it. I also started counting the stacks of money until I heard a man's voice outside. I knew that voice well, and I knew that it was my uncle Wimp's voice.

I tried to hurry and straighten things up, but I panicked, and created a bigger mess instead. I ran out the back door into our backyard pretending to be playing. The next thing I knew uncle Wimp was at the door telling me to come into the house. Once inside he got straight to it and asked me if I had been in his room. Now that threw me for a loop because

I'm thinking within myself... *Your room? When did you move in, and at what time did I get put out because I could've sworn that this was my room when I left for school this morning?*"

[Everyone bursts into laughter in the courtroom.]

"I was too scared to lie because there was no one there to put the blame on, so I accepted the responsibility for it. A swift smack sent bewilderment as pain came from the back of my head where he had slapped me. He told me not to come back into his room unless he told me to, and I agreed. That was my first exposure to drugs and money, but it wouldn't be my last.

Everybody that I knew, my brothers, cousins, and friends, all sold dope. It was all I ever saw, and it eventually became all that I ever did. We'll get deeper into that part of my story a little later. For the time being, I'd like to talk about how I ended up where I am now."

Chapter 3
History Lesson

"It was about three years ago that I found myself sitting in this very same courtroom facing Judge Ransom and Mr. Cain. I was looking at a very long time in prison. I had to face the exact same people I'm facing today, only now the roles are slightly different. The only thing that isn't the same is that I'm representing myself now. I don't have the same attorney that I had before.

The sentence that I faced was fifteen years to life. If I pleaded guilty, the lowest prison time I'd serve would be fifteen years. On the other hand, had I chosen to go to trial and lost, I'd be facing a maximum sentence of life in prison.

Now, I'm not sure what's going on in your minds right now, but as for myself, I'm thinking I was in a lose-lose type of situation. Without a shadow of a doubt I know that I've been through a lot in my life. I've been set up, robbed, and shot at a few times. But there's nothing, and I do mean nothing, that could send me running to God the way facing a life sentence would. It brought me to my knees and all I could do was call on the name of Jesus.

It was at that point in my life that I began to develop a deeper relationship with the Lord. Now I don't want you boys getting all worked up thinking I'm about to preach a sermon to you, but I'm not ashamed to give Jesus the glory for what he's done in my life. I'm not ashamed of my faith in him either.

I'll be totally honest with you guys. I don't know what this experience of doing time is like for you, but I do know what the experience of doing time is. I know what it feels like to regret a bad decision that seemed like it was the only logical choice you had at that time."

"I have a question to ask all of you."

"Which one of you is the oldest and who's the youngest?"

Two boys raise their hands as giggles permeates the room.

"Ok. Alright, I get it, Donnell exclaims. So, what's your name and how old are you, my man," he asks as he points at the youngster.

Pointing at himself, a puny teenager with low cut hair and ears that seem too large for his head says, "Are you talking to me?"

"Yeah, you raised your hand when I asked who was the youngest, right?"

The Compass of a Conscience

"Yes. My name is *Brandon Bright* and I'm sixteen."

"Sixteen, huh? So, what about you in the back of the room who raised your hand. What's your name and age?"

When this kid stood up, it was surprising to see his stature. He was about six feet five with reddish hair and completely covered with freckles. He kind of reminded Donnell of the little boy who played the sheriff's son on the Andy Griffin Show.

"My name is *Nisvet Ibricic*. and I'm eighteen," he says.

"You got a unique name and you're quite tall too, I see! Allow me to address the youngest. Brandon, I believe you said was your name, right? What is your understanding about the situation you're in right now?

"I really can't tell you too much about it. I've only been locked up for two months now but to me I've been locked up my whole life," Brandon replies.

"I don't want to sound rude or smart to you, but I don't view this situation as though I had a choice. If you ask me, I feel like this situation kinda chose me without my permission."

"What makes you say that?" Donnell asks.

"Not to offend you Mr. White, but you asked, and I can only keep it real with my answers. I pretty much have been on my own since I was born. I never really had a father and my mom ended up like he did. All I've had so far is Me, Myself, and I. You see the parents of my homies here today but the one thing you don't see is either one of my parents in attendance. You got your story and I got mine."

Donnell leans back in his chair and then leans forward. He pauses for a second to gather his thoughts, then says, "Wow, you got some issues that need to be dealt with before you self-destruct, my man."

"The one thing I can say is that I was kind of like you are now when I was your age. Sounds like you've come down with a condition often referred to as entitlement. Not to worry though, it's a condition that effects most people in a very common way.

Entitlement is when you think that you're owed or should receive something just based on your relationship to someone. I see you doing everything out of impulse like I used to do. I personally didn't think that anybody could teach me anything that I didn't already know or couldn't teach myself.

There's an old saying that if you keep doing what you're doing, you're gonna keep getting what you keep getting. I have found out that you can't live in this world all by yourself. We are all going to need somebody and you're no different. You just haven't realized that yet.

But it's ok. You just keep on living, young man, and I promise it'll come to you. If we both can agree on something it most likely will be that we both have our stories. Our common ground is that we can both respect each other's struggles."

"If you will allow me to, I'd like to share a story with you and everyone else in this courtroom this morning. It's about a man who has had his share of life's ups and downs. The thing is though, this guy refuses to allow the mistakes of his past to stop him from what he sees himself as in the future."

Chapter 4
One in the Same

This is a guy that I've practically known my whole life. His name is Moosey. We've shared so many similar experiences and have so much in common that you would probably think we are one in the same. Moosey's story impacted me deeply because I was given an up close and personal account of it, as it was told to me by Moosey.

As soon as Donnell finished with his introduction. An influx of memories began to invade his thoughts, and before he knew it, he was reliving the story as if it were happening for the first time.

Donnell started off by telling the group that Moosey was born prematurely on March 29, 1975. He went on to state that this day may not have any significant meaning to them, but for Moosey and his mother it was everything except normal. On this day, his mother Wanda Jean was taken to a local hospital called Sacred Heart, located in what was known then as "The Heights" of Pensacola, Fl.

All the strain and stress surrounding Wanda Jean's life at that time probably were a bit too much for her to handle. She was a 5 ft. 4 in. mother of two boys, with another child on the way. Wanda Jean's skin tone was dark brown, and she was married to a guy known to everyone as Lightning Wright. The couple separated due to an act of infidelity involving a man whom in Moosey's mind was a curse to the couple.

The man's name was Spoon and he was Moosey's father. There was nothing spectacular about Spoon according to Moosey's mother. Spoon wasn't that good looking of a man, but he had a little sense of style and a few dollars in his pockets. He had a way with words that seemed to be irresistible to most women.

Spoon's name became famous with the ladies for being known as a dog. He wasn't your average dog either. Spoon was a roaming dog, the kind that like to leave little puppies all over the place. Moosey's mom just so happened to be one of his victims back then. By the time she realized Spoon's true nature, he was long gone and so was her marriage to her husband Lightning.

She repeatedly tried to convince Spoon to reconsider his ways, but her pleading fell upon deaf ears it seemed. Spoon's treatment grew cold after impregnating her and wrecking her marriage. His response back then, were about as typical as any dead-beat dad today would use. Spoon rejected her and constantly proclaimed, "That ain't my baby."

On March 29th, Wanda Jean was desperate to find Spoon's whereabouts. She was determined to hold him accountable and to be a father to his child. After being told that he was now staying with his new girlfriend on the other side of town, she decided to pay them both a visit. When she arrived, she spotted Spoon's 1974 Cadillac Eldorado parked in the driveway close to the house. Without hesitation, she exited her vehicle, walked up the steps to the porch and started knocking on the door.

"May I help you?" The woman answering the door asked.

"I'm assuming it was the hormones from being pregnant that caused Wanda Jean to lose it and she began shouting "Spoon! Spoon! I know you can hear me calling your name. You might as well come on out here and deal with me and this baby you left me pregnant with. I'm going to make your life as miserable as you've made mine!"

The woman began cursing at Wanda Jean then, threatening her that if she didn't get off her property she was going to beat that baby right out of her. Almost immediately, a fight ensued and that's when Spoon did the unthinkable.

Just when you thought that Spoon couldn't get any lower than he already was, he did.

He exited the house to notice the two women fighting. They were pulling each other's hair, with Wanda Jean on top. Spoon tried to break the two up by prying their hands apart from each other's hair but was unsuccessful.

He yelled at Wanda Jean to let go of his girlfriend's hair, but she ignored him and that's when Spoon committed the most despicable act that a man can get himself involved in.

He snatched Wanda Jean by her head and her arms and, without hesitation, threw her pregnant body off the porch onto the ground below. To add insult to injury, while Wanda Jean lay on the front yard holding her stomach and crying in pain, she pleaded with Spoon and his girlfriend for help. And without any regard, they both ignored her cries, re-entered their home, and locked the door behind themselves.

It took the concern of some caring neighbors to call the paramedics and wait by Wanda Jean's side for them to arrive. The police and ambulance arrived and launched an investigation to inquire about what had happened. Both parties told their versions of what happened. After hearing both sides of the story, the police went with Wanda Jean's version. Spoon and his girlfriend were arrested on multiple counts of battery on Wanda Jean and aggravated battery on her unborn child.

Wanda Jean arrived at Sacred Heart Hospital in an ambulance around 3pm. The weather was very nice that spring day, but it appeared to have changed suddenly as it began to rain. Wanda Jean was quickly taken to the maternity ward. But all the while she was asking, "My baby is going to be ok, right?" To calm her down the doctors and nurses said whatever was necessary to placate her concerns.

Chapter 5
Special Delivery

The room that she was about to spend the next ten plus hours in was dimly lit. There were brown see-through curtains that added décor to the transparent hospital windows. She could see the rain thrusting hard on the glass and streaming slowly down as the nurse gave her an I.V.

Imagine how difficult it must have been for her. She was alone, pregnant, and travailing in labor. She had no husband or significant other by her side encouraging her to push when it was time to. Her parents weren't there to ease any of her fears by telling her that everything would be alright. She didn't even have a friend around to say, "Girl, you can do this, everything is going to be just fine."

Nope! She was there all alone for this experience.

The only comfort she had was the sound of beeping machines and monitors while nurses and doctors entered and exited the room. Life was quickly teaching this 25-year-old a lesson that she would never view the same again.

Minutes turned into hours, and the contractions began to worsen. A team of doctors entered the room. Wanda Jean began to panic and asked, "What's going on? Is there something wrong with my baby?"

"You're in labor and we're going to give you something to slow down your contractions." The doctor said politely.

"If that doesn't work we're going to have to go ahead and deliver this baby. Our concern is that you're only six months pregnant, and the baby's lungs and possibly other vital organs may not be fully developed."

Knowing that things were way more serious than what the doctor said, Wanda Jean resorted to the one thing that her mother always taught her to do as a child and that was to pray. Her faith in Jesus Christ seemed to have gotten rock solid quickly because she began to remember the scriptures she learned years ago that she thought she had forgotten.

Finally, after ten hours, this little soul decided it was time to reveal himself to the world. Given the circumstances, one might assume that another issue could've arisen, but it didn't. Left with no other alternative, the doctors had to give Wanda a cesarean birth and successfully delivered the baby.

The nurse took the tiny infant to an incubator and ran routine checks on him. Wanda Jean, though delirious from the medication she was given, frantically pleaded for information about her son.

The Compass of a Conscience

"Good job, Wanda. It's a boy," a nurse nearby said but the announcement gave Wanda Jean very little comfort as she gazed at the nurse with tear-filled eyes and asked, "Where is he? I want to see my child."

The nurse carefully placed the baby in Wanda Jean arms. As she lay there holding her son a nurse said, "He's somewhat of a miracle baby. Most preemie's don't do nearly as well. What's his name?"

Wanda Jean, without looking up or taking her eyes off her precious little baby, answered, "Moosey."

"Oh-Ke-Doe-ke the nurse said," with a confused look on her face.

The nurse immediately retrieved the baby from Wanda Jean and told her to allow the doctors time to give her son the care that he'll need. Thinking the worst, Wanda Jean started losing hope, but the effects of the anesthesia kicked in, putting her out like a lamp.

Two months passed by and little Moosey got up to five pounds and four ounces. Everything was well with him and the doctors were sending him home for the first time.

"That's the story of how the beginning could've very well have been the end for Moosey. His story doesn't end there though," says Donnell. Allow me to elaborate further...

The memories of Moosey's wonder years from the age of five to six well into his teenage years is a story struck with poverty. He wasn't poor, he was just plain "po". To add the letters "or" to the word would be giving him and his family a luxury that clearly didn't apply to them.

He was the middle child of five having four siblings consisting of four boys and one girl. His family lived in an area known as "*The Blocks*," located around the corner from A Street and Jackson St. in Pensacola, Fl. During those days Pensacola was nothing like the city it is today. It was more like an old-fashioned town then. The city was very industrious, hosting its very own port, paper and lumber mills. One might be led to believe that in a city where so many economic opportunities were present, that this place would be the ideal breeding ground for jobs but that wasn't the case at that time.

There literally were two class of citizens around during that time. You had the upper class and the other class. The upper class were the people who were well off and always seemed to be the most natural fit for better employment. Then there was the other class of people, the minority or poor citizens who found it extremely rare to even have a job that pays them, let alone one to support a family with. If you are wondering about a middle class, there was not even a hint or sprinkle of it back in those days.

The Compass of a Conscience

To be a minority proved to be more of a disability than anything because even at the cost of ten cents, public transportation was just too expensive for most minorities. So, walking was Moosey's family's only option. They walked everywhere, no matter what the weather was; be it rain, sleet, or snow. They walked.

The commute from the nicer neighborhoods where the rich people resided to the poor communities, where Moosey and his family lived, was quite the experience for him.

As they would walk through the rich and predominantly white neighborhoods they'd see all kinds of cool stuff like beautiful homes, nice cars, amazing toys, well-manicured trees, and the greenest lawns.

Their community parks looked like Disneyland to Moosey as he passed by them. They were such a delightful sight to his little eyes that he forgot how sore and tired his legs and feet were from walking. It wasn't until he was leaving the wealthy district and approached the poor district or the *Slums*, which were predominantly black, that the journey became unbearable for him.

In his mind, it was as if they had traded in the clear blue skies for a dark and rainy day. The roads were unpaved and riddled with potholes. There were broken down shotgun houses with fences barely standing that leaned in either direction, with sections missing from them. Yards were engulfed with red clay and wild grass that grew sporadically in patches, trees were rotten to the root. There were cars sitting on all four flats that had been abandoned for years. This is just a mild portrait of the poverty level of these communities during that era.

At his age, the one thing that was absolutely mind blowing for Moosey to see was the unity that existed among black people back in those days. Yes, he found it fascinating to see all the expensive things as he walked through the rich districts, but he instantly noticed that there was a void in those communities that was plentiful in the poor community.

Now I'm not speaking about money or cosmetics either.

The difference I'm speaking of is in the quality of life. It became more apparent to him as he passed through the wealthy neighborhoods that the people who lived there weren't very neighborly. The appearance on their faces sported curious looks and frowns that left Moosey with the impression that they weren't very nice or even happy people at all.

On the other hand, what was cemented into his mind as he walked through the poor communities that he lived in was how happy and friendly everyone was. Whether they knew you personally or not, you couldn't pass a single home without getting a "Hey there, how ya'll doin dis evening?" from the elderly men, or a "Hey shuga!" from the elderly women sitting on their porch in a swing or in a rocking chair.

What impressed him the most was although the park was missing swings, its basketball court completely covered with glass, and had only one beat up rim to play hoops, you could always hear the echoes of children's laughter all day. To them nothing was missing or wrong with their environment.

The essence of joy and contentment filled the air, which had not existed in those rich neighborhoods. So much so, that on any given day you could hear the song *"Love and Happiness,"* by the Rev. Al Green blasting from someone's stereo as you passed by their home or from a car, blaring from its speakers. The way the community pulled together to help one another back in those days baffled Moosey in comparison to the way things are today."

Chapter 6
Disaster Strikes

Growing up without financial security causes tremendous strains on families. In Moosey's childhood days there wasn't a daycare on every corner like there is nowadays.

Neighbors were very much engaged with each-others' affairs. Mothers and fathers could leave their children at home by themselves and ask their neighbors to keep an eye out for them. That was the only option available to most parents and Moosey's family was no exception to the rule.

The children from oldest to youngest were Sylvester, Julius, Moosey, Kenny and Lakeisha. The one thing you can be sure of, is that the youngest child always got the most attention and accompanied mommy wherever she went. On the other hand, if you were a toddler that could walk and talk, chances were, you got left at home with your other siblings.

It was on the eve of a cold winter night in October 1980 that Moosey and his family's lives traumatically changed.

His mother Wanda Jean, as she had done many times before, left the boys at home alone. She took their little sister with her to church. She left Sylvester in charge to watch over his little brothers and she made him repeat to her what to do and where to go in case of an emergency.

She put the boys to sleep and left for church. It turned out to be a decision she'd regret the for rest of her life.

The house they lived in was a shotgun house with a huge silver painted gas tank adjacent to it. The steps that led up to the wooden porch of the house were rotten and unstable but still standing nonetheless. The exterior of the house itself was made mostly of wood covered with some shingle-like material.

The roof was layered with sheets of tin that were so severely rusted that the rust dust, as they used to call it, continually fell inside like snow.

As you entered the house you were greeted by a very small living room that played host to an antique cast iron couch with worn out pillows on it. To the right of it, a small television sat on the floor with antennas standing upright and the tips of them wrapped in aluminum foil. In plain view from there was the kitchen and from the kitchen there appeared a hallway where a gas operated space heater stood. Two bedrooms positioned across from each other were at the end of the hallway.

Most of the houses in those days were hand-built by hardworking resourceful men and women who made *do* with whatever materials they could scrape together. Due to a lack of insulation, houses built like this, would get extremely cold during the winter.

From the moment Moosey began to tell me about this tragic event, I could see tears forming in his eyes. For me, that was an indication that this wasn't going to be an average story.

Turns out it would become one of the most heart-wrenching stories I'd ever heard. It would remind me of a similar personal experience that occurred in my life. On that fateful winter night in October 1980, Moosey was awakened by the extremely cold temperatures of the house. He could see his younger brother Kenny lying next to him. Sylvester, his oldest brother, was lying on a blanket on the floor next to Kenny, fast asleep. Moosey rolled over then on his left expecting to see his other brother, but to his surprise he wasn't there, or even in the room at all.

Out of pure curiosity, he sprang up off the floor in search of him. He walked out of the bedroom into the hallway where he noticed his brother kneeling on the other end of the hallway in front of the heater. He must have startled his brother the closer he got to him because, the box of sticks his brother was holding flew up into the air and little sticks began flying all over the place, when he heard Moosey's voice.

"What are you doing?" Moosey asked his brother.

"I'm trying to make this heater work. It's cold in here," his brother replied while gathering and picking up the sticks.

"I'm cold too, Moosey said," as he pitched in to help round up the scattered sticks.

After picking up a few of the sticks it didn't take Moosey long to figure out that the sticks were matches.

Moosey remembered his mother warning them about playing with matches. Moreover, the discipline that was to follow if they ever got caught doing so. He cautions his brother.

"Ooooh! You know mamma gon' beat the mess outta you. You know we ain't supposed to play with no matches," Moosey told his brother.

"Shut up!", his brother said with a look of frustration on his face. "I ain't doin nothing but lighting this heater."

He took out a match and struck it along the side of the box and watched it burn down to his fingertips. His brother repeated the demonstration a few more times before Moosey was enticed, and joined in. The two of them got so involved with their little experiment, that they almost burned every match in the box.

Now, they began to realize they were in big trouble and they feared the discipline coming their way. Their mother used those matches to light the stove and everything else in the house. There was no way she wouldn't notice the matches all burned up. The low temperatures of the house caused them to refocus their efforts back to their original mission. That was getting the heater to work.

Moosey told me that he must have seen his mother and other adults light that heater with matches a million times. What him and his brother were unaware of is that the adults were only lighting the pilot light. It seemed so simple to them but what they were too young to understand was that they were on the verge of a major catastrophe.

They lit up one match and stuck it in the side of the heater and all hell broke loose.

Everything happened so fast and the next thing they knew, they were outside of their house. There they were, three little boys standing in the street, gazing in astonishment of the fire raging inside of their house. They could hear the cracking sounds piercing through the imagery of the flames. It was a very frightening thing to watch. The smoke was so dark and thick that even in the shadow of the night you could clearly see it and feel the smothering heat coming from it.

Moosey began hearing the voices of his neighbors, running and screaming frantically towards his house asking, "Where's Wanda Jean and her kids?" Once they could see the kids amidst the crowd, the concerned onlookers inquired

The Compass of a Conscience

about their mother's whereabouts. Sylvester wasn't quite as responsive as Moosey and their other brother who was with them. He just kept repeating, almost in a murmur, "Kenny's in there asleep." By that time the three of them were surrounded by people. Sylvester must have repeated it enough times that it finally dawned on a few folks because they began to ask him.

"Kenny who? What are you trying to tell us, baby?" A woman asked.

"My little brother," Sylvester said.

It was at that moment the peace of mind everyone seemingly had, collapsed, and shock kicked in. Adding more drama to an already severe situation. Sylvester, being the courageous ten-year-old he was, fearlessly charged toward the burning house, and entered. Everything just spiraled out of control by then. Cumbersome would describe the hopelessness of the crowd.

Not only was Kenny's life at stake but Sylvester's life was in danger now as well. The entire situation had reached its lowest level at this point.

The cries of "Oh my God, please don't let them babies die!" seemed to become the focal theme and emotional state of everyone that dreadful night. In the distance, everyone could hear the echoes of sirens approaching, and the closer they got the more deafening the sound became. Moosey's focus momentarily were on the firefighters, paramedics, and the Police Department, as he watched them all get set up.

Paranoia started to creep in because people began latching onto Moosey and his brother to prevent them from going back into the house, putting more lives at risk. The scene appeared to be one of complete chaos, at least in Moosey's mind it did. As his little eyes scanned around, people were giving each agency their knowledge of the situation and urging them to act quickly.

Kenny and Sylvester both had been in the house for some time now. Their chances of survival were slim considering the dire nature of the situation. Even back then all first responders were mandated to follow strict protocol in case of an emergency. The intent was to minimize the risk of death for themselves and the public. However, protocol has no significance when the lives of children are on the line.

Based on the severity of this situation just about anyone would rise to the occasion to save the life of a child. On this night, a firefighter and a hero lost his life to save the lives of two kids he'd never met before.

His name was Ralph Fleetman, a thirty-one-year-old Caucasian male. He was a devoted father with children around the same ages as Moosey and his brothers. The brave fireman sprang into action and entered the fiery house in search of the children. The house was completely engulfed in flames and nobody had any real hope of a positive outcome, until Ralph emerged holding what appeared to be a lifeless body and handed it over to the paramedics standing by.

It was the most horrific sight Moosey had ever seen.

The outcry from everyone around was overwhelming. There, lying motionless on the stretcher was Sylvester, unrecognizable. It looked as if someone had skinned him alive. Where natural skin once was, there was now raw flesh mingled with blood. The smell was unlike anything Moosey had ever smelled before. Ralph the firefighter's courageous efforts didn't end there, for he entered the house a second time to search for Kenny. By this time Moosey's mother had arrived on the scene.

One could only imagine what was going through her mind seeing the condition of her ten-year-old son, plus being informed that her four-year-old, whom most at the scene believed to already be dead due to the prolonged exposure, was still trapped inside.

What Moosey saw next was something he said he'll always have nightmares about for as long as he lives. His mom started sprinting towards their burning house and it was as if an evil spirit or something had taken control of the house that night.

As Moosey recalls it, his mom made her way to the first step of the porch and an angry cloud of smoke came out to meet her. The sound coming from it was like a loud growl or something. It completely covered his mother and he just screamed and cried. Just as fast as it hit her it was gone, leaving his mother unconscious on the ground.

Even more heart-stopping of an experience that night for Moosey's mom was regaining consciousness just in time to see Ralph emerging with what everyone knew was Kenny's body. As soon as their silhouettes began to break the plane of the house entrance, the entire structure caved in suddenly, killing them both.

"Lord, No! My baby... Kenny! Kenny!" screamed Moosey's mom.

She broke loose from the individuals who had resuscitated her, and sprinted toward the house again. She just fell to the ground in disbelief. Slightly, burning her arms in the fire surrounding the site where her house once stood. The Fire Department finally extinguished the fire.

Moosey's mother, after receiving medical attention for her injuries, faced the most difficult reality that any parent has ever had to deal with. That had to be one of the darkest nights ever for Moosey's family. It forever altered so many lives on many different levels.

In summary, a mother loses one of her children and nearly loses another almost simultaneously, not to mention losing every possession she ever owned__" Pictures, Identification, you name it, gone up in flames. Without losing her sanity she had to identify the charred remains of her four-year-old son, and at the same time pull herself together to be by her ten-year-old son's side, who was fighting for his life.

Sylvester was burned over seventy percent of his body, but by the grace of God he miraculously survived. Moosey knew without a shadow of a doubt that Ralph Fleetman was a guardian angel sent by God. Ralph was someone's husband, he was a father, also a son, and albeit it led to his own demise, he was sent to save Sylvester's life. Sylvester lived on to see the age of 30 years old before passing away.

Darnell D Wright

Sylvester T Wright - Rest in Heaven

This Chapter is Dedicated to the Memory of Sylvester "Sly" Wright

Chapter 7
Guilty Conscience

At that point of Moosey telling me his story, I noticed that he dropped his head and a dead silence filled the air. He looked me square in the eyes and said, "You know what Donnell? Telling you this is extremely difficult for me because of how guilty I feel. I was only five or six years old when all this took place but somehow I feel like I'm to blame for what happened to my brothers." He told me that he'd vowed never to forget what had happened that dreadful night.

Wisely, I took a few minutes to digest all I had heard before I engaged anymore conversation out of him. My thoughts at the time was, I didn't want to say the wrong thing that could heighten the grief already brewing inside of him. But as soon as I uttered the words, "It's gonna be alright brother," he burst into tears saying, "I killed my little brother! I should've died in that house fire, since I'm the one who started it. Why did he have to die, and I get to live?"

It was at that very moment that I began to realize how we can sweep things under the rug for many years to avoid dealing with them. Once rehashed it has the same impact on us as it did when it first occurred. The only words that came to my mind were, "Brother, it's not your fault. You were a child and as children we make mistakes.

You and your brother did no different than any other children in your shoes would have done. I don't blame you and nobody else in their right mind would.

If there's any blame to pass around it should be to the circumstances surrounding your life. There's so much I see wrong about everything that happened to you and your family. Poverty is at the helm of the issue that surrounds most of us all our lives.

My understanding of poverty is that it's a state of mind that can easily become a state of being. Being born into poverty didn't give us much of a chance. Most of the time as kids we only saw momma and grandma struggling with no male presence in the home.

Moosey concluded that the community was deeply impacted by this tragedy and showed compassion for his family's loss. So much so that the number of mourners who attended Kenny's funeral was so great that the church where it was held couldn't seat them all. Most of the mourners that stood without, had to look through the windows of the church. This would be Moosey's first inauguration to death and funerals, but not his last."

The Compass of a Conscience

R.I.H- Kenny Jerome Wright
This is an actual photo of Kenny, Age-4
This photo is the sole surviving relic of the house fire that claimed his life.

Love is Taught
Love is Learned
Love can be Patient
and wait it's Turn
Love likes to Give
Hardly ever it Takes
As Real as it gets
LOVE'S NEVER FAKE!
Pure like the lyrics
Of a beautiful song
When the heartbeat has
stopped
Forever Love will live on...

- **Darnell Wright**

Chapter 8
Recess

Immediately after telling Moosey's story, Donnnell revert his attention back to Brandon. The kid he was telling it to.

"Life is short and way too precious to be bogged down with unforgiveness Brandon. I can see the load that you're carrying young man and I guarantee you that it is too big of a burden for you. The truth of the matter is bearing the weight of the world is impossible for anybody to endure, much less a child such as yourself. I've learned that just because society has dealt me a bad hand, I can't just throw in the towel. I must play the hand I've been dealt. I use my personal experiences like a deck of stacked cards. I'm trying to ensure myself a better hand now than what I had before.

Life is the same way, Brandon. Make use of the life you have by first changing the way you think and the people you surround yourself with. If you use the skills you have, you can develop a trump card-like strategy for every situation you go through.

Remember, once you become the dealer the odds are always in your favor. All I'm asking is for you not to quit on yourself. The only thing that could ever beat a failure was a try. If you're trying, failure is not an option.

Five minutes of silence permeate the courtroom before Judge Ransom said, "Brandon, tell us your thoughts and how you feel about what Mr. White just said to you."

"To be honest, Judge, that was kinda deep what Mr. White was saying. Sometimes when you think you got it bad someone else has it worse. What he said about his friend really touched me. I'm thinking hard on what he asked me to do, prior to him telling the story, and that was to listen. I can say that I'm glad I did. I might be young and hard-headed but I'm not stupid. Getting locked up was a dumb move on my part.

No one has ever sat me down and really explained things to me the way he did, at least no one I could relate to. I was only told where and how my life would end up. I don't know, I guess I'm finally starting to get that it's not always about what's being said. Sometimes it's the one who's saying it that makes the difference. I felt Mr. White's pain listening to his friend tell him about his life and that lets me know that he ain't no square. He done been through some thangs and he's real. There's not many people I can vibe with or listen to, but I feel him."

"Wow!! Judge Ransom said, that was a powerful endorsement you gave Mr. White, Brandon."

Donnell interjects and says, "Really, Your Honor, that was only a fraction of Moosey's story. I have so much more that I can share about his life, but I'm aware that time is an issue this morning, so I'll end it there."

"Oh no, Mr. White, Judge Ransom aggressively responds. We're all here for one reason. I believe it takes someone like you to get through to these boys. I'm not the one to impede on progress and I'm not putting a muzzle over the wisdom you're sharing. You are free to proceed, but before you do let me ask is there anyone that needs a bathroom break?"

After getting a split reaction to her question, Judge Ransom decides to take a fifteen-minute recess.

Chapter 9
What A Lady

As occupants start exiting the courtroom, an eerie sound of silence fills the room. A frail elderly African-American woman extends a withered hand to touch the arm of a staff member of Ohallowbee, who whispers a few words with the old woman and then beckons for the assistance of a U.S. Marshall standing nearby. The Marshall talks briefly with the two of them and then walks over, kneels beside Donnell, and informs him that an elderly lady has a few questions to ask him.

Donnell nods and says it is ok for her to ask him her questions. Then, he turns and asks, "What would you like to ask me, ma'am?"

"My name is Lucy. How you doin today, baby?" The old lady asks.

"I'm doing pretty good, Mrs. Lucy. How about yourself?"

"Oh shuga, when you get to be my age it ain't no longer bout how you doin, but rather how you been living. Once you live to be my age you just flip the pages of the calendar, honey. It's about how you treat folks. I ain't neva been in your shoes and of course I ain't neva been to jail before either, but I do feel sorry for you and even more for these here babies following in your footsteps. You understand what I'm trying to say to ya, darlin?"

"Yes, ma'am, I do," Donnell says.

"I'll be turning 86 years old in a few days and it's only by the grace of God that I can still walk right and talk good. Even though my children don't like it, I drive myself wherever I want to when I want to. I'm here to tell you, honey, that I don't need nobody but Jesus."

"You hear me," Mrs. Lucy says.

Donnell chuckles and says, "I know that's right, momma."

"That's my grandbaby Mario sitting on the end over yonder. Can you see him? He the one with all that hair on his face. Now, I know he look like a man but really he just a little 'Ol' boy. I don't know how many times I done told that boy to cut all that mess off his face and mouth, but you know how they are. You can't teach them nothing that they don't already know. When our daughter dropped him off on my husband and me, boy I tell ya, we had a time raising that boy. That child was so hard-headed that all you could do was scream, "Man!" sometimes. Most of the time you'd have to say it twice to keep from cursing the little fella out. That's how he got his nickname *Man-Man,* because we had to repeat it so much."

The Compass of a Conscience

[Giggles and laughter erupt throughout the courtroom.]

"You know, I've been sitting here listening to all the things that you been saying. It's good to hear it come from a man who done been through what these boys might have to go through if they keep this mess up. I appreciate the way you tell them like it is, that's good baby. Don't hold your tongue back on their butts because then they'll lose respect for you. They don't know it yet that life ain't nothing to play with. I just can't help but to wonder what happened to *Moochie*, I believe is his name that you've been talking about?"

Donnell responds, "Thanks for the nice words, Mrs. Lucy. You know, listening to you got me thinking about Ms. Moe. You kinda remind me of her, Mrs. Lucy."

"Who is Ms. Moe, baby?" Mrs. Lucy asks.

"She was Moosey's grandmother," Donnell replies.

"Much like the situation you have going with your grandson, Mario. Moosey's grandmother played a vital role in raising him. She was known to everyone as Ms. Moe. I was very inspired by hearing him tell the story of his relationship with his grandmother. Especially the confidence he displayed when saying he was raised by women. Moosey credits the wisdom he gained to the powerful influence of the women in his life. He told me that after his little brother Kenny's death his family moved in with his grandmother.

Ms. Moe was a short woman with a wide frame. Her dark skin complexion made her head of completely grey hair look mysteriously white. If there was anything about her that was an expression of her character, it was to be found in the collection of wigs she had.

She had a wig readily accessible on the heads of styrofoam mannequins for all occasions, it seemed. They all stayed puffed, permed, curled, pressed and ready to go.

Her style of fashion, however, was matched more to her everyday approach to life. She was a workaholic. Ms. Moe always wore her work uniforms, which had big buttons going from her neck to her knees. On both sides of her uniform were huge pockets. Each uniform she wore had a patch bearing her name, compliments of her employer.

She was best known for her fiery and zero tolerance temper. Her temper was one to be respected because she carried around a nickel-plated 22 caliber pistol in those big pockets of hers. Everybody in the neighborhood understood how she handled conflict. It was a rare thing to see Ms. Moe's hands. That's because they stayed in her uniform pockets close to her pistol. She had no problems with letting her pistol end an argument. She stayed ready to do whatever, to whomever, whenever she needed to.

However, there was another side of her that revealed how loving she was. She ran a soup kitchen out of that little shotgun house of hers. Homeless folk and drunks wandered in from the streets to get a plate and a little prayer. She grew a great deal of her food in her garden on the side of her house.

Moosey's admiration for his grandmother to me was quite impressive but he didn't always feel that way. His mother had to explain to him his grandmother's perspective on life, slowly but sure enough he got use to her unorthodox way of doing things.

Living with his grandmother was like being in a work slash religious boot camp. You'd be fast asleep and then awakened around 3:30am by the sound of Ms. Moe singing old Gospel songs, beating on an old drum and praying aloud. She also had to anoint the foreheads of everyone in the house with blessed oil.

I remember laughing so hard when Moosey said that the blessed oil kept his forehead greasy all-day long. This routine of hers generally lasted up to an hour. If you were lucky you got a few minutes of sleep in before being awakened again around 5 to 5:30am. She'd load Moosey and his brothers into her 1981 Chevy El Camino to go to downtown Pensacola and dig through dumpsters looking for aluminum cans.

In her own words she called it, *A side hustle to make some extra money.*

Of course, the boys didn't see it that way at all. They looked at it as an inhumane thing for anybody to have to endure. She was in her late fifties when Moosey's mom moved in. Physically, Ms. Moe couldn't climb in and out of any dumpsters. So, the boys' youth worked wonders to make the impossible possible.

After being spared from this dirty job because he was the youngest, Moosey's luck finally ran out and he got drafted for duty. His grandmother ordered him to go into the dumpster, and to start tearing open trash bags and sorting through them.

His first time in the dumpster proved to be even more horrible of an experience than he imagined it would be. There were all kinds of very nasty liquids in there including spit, feces, and other contaminated fluids. He said that the smell leading up to and inside of the dumpster was absolutely, breathtaking.

To make matters worse, the cheap flashlight that they were using stopped working. The darkness of the container made Moosey panic and he wanted out. The only thing that he could see was the square entrance by which he got into the dumpster. So, he began to make his way quickly towards it stepping on and over trash bags beneath him.

He was just about to reach the opening when he lost his balance. Everything kinda went wrong after that. He felt

The Compass of a Conscience

himself losing his balance so, he immediately stuck his arms out to prevent getting hurt. When his hands slid down the slime covered walls things really went downhill from there. You can just about imagine what followed next?

Yep, his face!!!

Using the clean areas of his shirt to wipe the slime off his face was an experience that left him feeling dirty and disgusted. He knew that he couldn't complain or say anything because he feared what Ms. Moe would say. At best, all that he could do was just stand there with tears running down his face.

His intuition was right on the money because he recalls Ms. Moe asking him.

"What ail you boy? I know you betta fix yo face before I give you something to really cry about. It ain't nothing that a little soap and water can't get off. You acting like you almost got killed or something. The more you stay around me I'm gon break you out of that sissy stuff and make a man of you, you watch!"

Those words became the law and five days a week at that. On Saturdays, they had to get up extra early to crush the cans they collected, bag and then load the bags onto the back of her El Camino. All three of the brothers had to go with her to the local scrap yard where she would sell them.

Ms. Moe wanted to get to the scrapyard before anyone else did to avoid the long lines. She made about $80.00 on a slow week and as much as $300 when she had a good week. Moosey and his brothers always got the same ten bucks and a complimentary breakfast courtesy of grandma's tab.

Their schedule became so routine that they began to mock and recite to one another what she thought of as a motivational speech, which went sort of like this:

"I'm trying to raise ya'll boys to be men. I believe that a man should always have a few extra dollars in his pockets to support his family and himself. What I'm trying to teach you boys is how to have a side hustle to make money. You'll never go broke when you know that there are plenty of ways to make a dollar. If there's one thing that momma can't stand is a sorry man, because a man has the strength to work hard like a mule.

Momma ain't got no respect for no broke woman either. She might not have the strength of a man but common-sense ought to let her know that she was born with money and she sits on it every day.

I know you boys too young to understand what that might mean but long as y'all keep rising up in the morning it'll all make sense to ya, by and by. Momma ain't gon' always be around to give ya'll this lesson for free and ain't *nobody gone give you nothing for free. You gotta look out for yourself. Do y'all understand me?"*

Whether they agreed or disagreed their response was always, "Yes, Ma'am."

Thinking back on it, in her own unusual way Ms. Moe was teaching them how to survive the only way that she knew how to.

Chapter 10
Cut from a different Cloth

Now, I know that there may be some of you who might be thinking that Ms. Moe's methods of raising her grandchildren were unusual or even crazy, but before you judge please allow me to share a little about her religious beliefs and upbringing.

Throughout her life, Ms. Moe has had to deal with poverty, racial injustices and violence. As a widow and a single mother, her only concern was providing for her family. Facing those obstacles as a black woman was tantamount to the survival instincts she developed. What was most interesting was the story of how she ended up in Pensacola, Florida.

She was born and raised in Selma, Alabama and grew up thinking that her sister Leola, was her mother. She was the youngest of her mother's five children and her mother died from complications while giving birth to her. It was said that Leola resented her and secretly blamed her for their mother's death, so she was extremely hard on Ms. Moe.

Ms. Moe was forced into child labor and worked alongside Leola. She began *croppin baca*, or picking tobacco at the tender age of five years old. She worked from sunrise to sunset and did so until she was a teenager. Due to an unavoidable event that occurred when she only fifteen years old. The course of Ms. Moe's life would ultimately be changed.

Leola sent her down the trail, as they were accustomed to calling it, to go get food for supper. Along the route she encountered a white man twice her age, whom she knew very well. She knew him well because he had a unique association to her family. After having brief conversation with her, he attempted to force himself on Ms. Moe.

Her brother just so happened to be coming down the trail and he saw what was happening to his little sister. Quickly scanning the area, he spots a stick. With the intent of killing, he hits the guy in the head with it. Then, he grabbed Ms. Moe and they ran home to tell Leola about what just happened.

It turns out that the guy he hit was the owner of the tobacco field in which their family worked. Leola was worried and afraid for their lives, as well as her own. Hoping to avoid any retaliation from anyone related to or even the tobacco field owner himself, Leola sent them away and they settled in Pensacola, Florida.

In Pensacola, they had no family and didn't know anyone. They did what they naturally had instincts to do, and that was to survive. Ms. Moe married her husband, who was twice her age. He was a deacon at the church she attended. She was barely sixteen when they got married.

Amazingly, she taught herself how to read and write from reading and studying the bible every day. She would ask anyone who was available what certain words were, what they meant, and how to pronounce them.

Knowing this kind of information gives you a better understanding of just how amazing this lady really was. She was a warrior and her sayings and wisdom live on through her children and grandchildren. It was those early morning prayers of hers that Moosey remembered the most. Her devotion to Christ was acknowledgement that only He could provide for and take care of her and her family.

Brandon, the kid who Donnell earlier had seemed to have made a connection with raises his hand.

"Yes, Brandon. You have a question?"

"So, what happened to the tobacco field owner? Did Ms. Moe's brother kill him?"

"That I rather not discuss, young man. The only reason that I feel comfortable sharing this story especially in an environment like this is because she's deceased now, and nothing can be done about it at this point anyway. I hope that something in this story gives you encouragement, Mrs.

Lucy, to continue to support and pray for your grandson. He's gonna need it. Your grandson may not be where you think he should be, but somehow God has put him where he needs to be. He now has the time to sit back and reflect on the decisions he's made."

Darnell D Wright

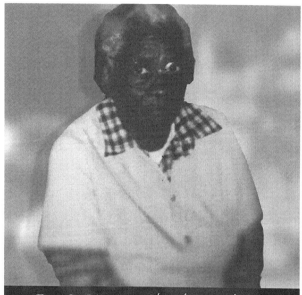

Rest In Heaven: Claudia Pearl Moore

TIME AFTER TIME...

Time only responds to time
Are the reflections of my mind
Memories left unconscious
God awakens from time to time
The mirror reflects a reflection
Be it your reflection or be it mine
Time will not bring back my granny
and she will not bring back the Time....

- Darnell Wright

Chapter 11
Freedom

"All Rise. The Honorable Stacy Ransom presiding. Maintain order in the court."

Judge Ransom takes her seat and says, "You may be seated."

"Before I proceed with sentencing this case, my apologies for the lengthy recess. I'm aware that 15 minutes turned into 45 minutes can seem like forever when you're waiting for a verdict. My assistant was checking to confirm some pertinent information about this case at my request. Mr. White, I must say that in my field I've seen and just about heard it all. Rarely does a case come along that has given me this much difficulty to preside over. Each day I sit on this bench listening to spouses pleading with the court on behalf of a loved one and mothers crying.

I have one of the toughest jobs on the planet, but I chose this profession and I wouldn't be worthy to wear my robe if I didn't uphold the law. It's just what I do. I've wrestled with your case and struggled to impose a sentence that would be both fair and serve in the best interests of justice. With that said, I am ready to move forward with sentencing and I hereby impose the following sentence:

On count one, possession of a controlled substance with the intent to distribute, I sentence you to serve a term of 120 months - ten years of imprisonment - to the custody of the Federal Bureau of Prisons, followed by a term of 60 months - five years of supervision after your release from custody.

On count two, possession of a firearm by a convicted felon, I sentence you to serve a term of 120 months - ten years - of imprisonment in the custody of the Federal Bureau of Prisons followed by a term of 60 months - five years of supervision after your release from custody - to run consecutively to count one.

You are hereby ordered to be in the custody of The Federal Bureau of Prisons for a term of imprisonment totaling 220 months - 20 years - to be followed by a term of supervision totaling 120 months - ten years- to run consecutively for each count. Has your attorney discussed and explained to you what your sentence is and do you understand your sentence here today, Mr. White?"

"Yes, I understand, Your Honor."

"Very well then. At this time, I am suspending both sentences and imposing the following sanctions on you. As to count one, possession of a controlled substance with the intent to distribute, I will credit you with time served and I hereby sentence you to a term of 60 months - five years- of supervision. On count two, possession of a firearm by a

The Compass of a Conscience

convicted felon, I will credit you with time served and I hereby sentence you to a term of 60 months - five years - of supervision. Count two is to run concurrent to count one. I adjudicate you guilty but suspend each sentence imposed without prejudice."

"Mr. White, you will be transported back to the jail to be released. I wish you success"

"Thank You Jesus," one of Donnell's relatives shouts out.

"Maintain order in the court," a Marshall says authoritatively.

"One more thing," says Judge Ransom.

"Mr. White, I'm convinced that you are seeking a second chance and you've received it here today. I want you to know that I've rolled the dice on you today in hopes that I don't crap out. Not only will I, yourself and your family be liable but society in whole will pay the penalty if this decision turns out to be a mistake.

The last thing I want you to remember is that just like there's a penalty to pay when you crap out at the casino, reprehensible consequences will apply if I ever see you in my courtroom again. There will no mercy left to give, are we clear," Judge Ransom asks.

"Yes, Your Honor. I understand," Donnell White replies.

"Well, I wish you luck. I believe this was our last case on the docket for today, so court is adjourned."

"*All rise...*" the court's Marshall says.

Chapter 12
The Offer

The staff of the Ohallowbee Detention Center for Boys starts removing the detainees from the courtroom. A soft-spoken member of the staff then approaches Donnell and says, "Hello, Mr. White. My name is Eunice. I am a social worker and a counselor for Ohallowbee. You have a natural ability to capture a person's attention, especially our boys. I, for one, have never seen them so focused and attentive to what anyone ever had to say. But they sure listened to you today. Would you be interested in volunteering as a mentor to the boys at our facility?"

Before Donnell could respond she adds, "It's not a paying gig because its volunteer based. So, of course we understand that it will be at your leisure. You set the times and dates and we'll make the necessary adjustments."

"Sure," Donnell replies.

"Awesome," Eunice says.

"Here's my card. You can call me when you're released. I look forward to possibly working with you, Mr. White. Hopefully you can influence the boys to see the need to change their lives. Maybe even a blueprint for them on becoming productive and successful individuals."

"One never knows?" says Donnell.

The ride back to Holcomb County Jail seems like one big daydream to Donnell.

"Did what just happened, really happen back there in court today?" He asks his transporters as he is sitting, shackled, in disbelief.

"Am I a free man or is my imagination running wild on me?"

"Oh, it happened," one of his transporters says. "But you're not quite in the clear yet. We'll have to run a final warrant check on you before we can release you."

They pull into the Holcomb County Jail authorized vehicle only entrance. There, they stop in front of a metal door and wait for it to lift. The door lifts and leads them into the Sally Port as they drive in.

Once inside, they open the vehicle's back door to assist Donnell in getting out. Donnell notices that their routine this time though is different from the last time. Instead of taking him back to his cell, he's placed inside a holding cell located in central booking. There he remains while waiting for warrants to clear.

The Compass of a Conscience

Eight hours later, a correctional officer yells "White, Donnell White!"

"Yeah," he replies.

"Report to medical when I buzz you out."

Without hesitation, Donnell jumps up when he hears the buzzer and exits the cell. The nurse on duty requests his signature for release forms and sends him back to central booking where a sergeant is waiting for him. The sergeant escorts him to the fingerprinting room and Donnell asks nervously, "Do I have a warrant?"

The officer does not respond to him. Instead, he instructs him to place his hand on the fingerprint scanner. Afterwards, the sergeant informs Donnell that he will be taken back to his cell to gather his belongings and be brought back to central booking thereafter to arrange pick up for himself. His escorts are instructed to take him to his cell. He wastes no time packing the things that are of importance to him. In the giving nature of his character, he gives his remaining commissary and other items to less fortunate inmates who are in need.

The Correctional officers allow him a few extra minutes to say his goodbye's before escorting him back to central booking to arrange pickup. Donnell makes his phone call, and to his surprise, family members are already on standby in the jail lobby.

The ride home from the jail is joyous and overloaded with questions from family members. Donnell is trying hard to enjoy his newly found freedom but for some strange reason he feels this huge void in his life.

Chapter 13
A Fresh Start

Days later he reports to his parole officer to start supervision. Towards the end of his visit, his parole officer gives him a business card. The card is from Eunice Eaton the counselor who approached him from Ohallowbee Detention Center for Boys. When he sees the name on the card, a feeling of gratitude comes over him and he says, "Lord Jesus, I thank you."

From that moment on, he couldn't wait to get out of the parole officer's office and call Ms. Eaton. After being cleared to leave by his parole officer, he walks at a very fast pace to his vehicle and calls Ms. Eaton immediately. On the first attempt, he gets her voicemail. He tries calling back and, while in the middle of leaving her a message, her number comes across on the other line. He cuts his message short and clicks over to answer.

"Hi, this is Eunice Eaton. I see that someone from this number tried to reach me and I was returning their call."

"Hi Eunice, this is Donnell White. I just received your card from my parole officer, Mr. Avis. I didn't forget about your offer. It's just that I've been busy adjusting back into society."

"Oh, there's no need to explain yourself to me, Mr. White. Trust me, I understand. I just wanted to touch base with you to be sure that you had my info, just in case you misplaced it somewhere somehow. So, does this call confirm the possibility of you joining us soon?" Ms. Eaton asks.

Donnell replies, "Yes, that's exactly what it means and I'm hoping that this phone call will speed things up."

"It most definitely will, Mr. White!" Eunice answers back. "This is awesome news and I know that you will have a huge impact on the boys."

"I can't wait to get started!" Donnell exclaims. "Speaking of, when can I start?"

"Well, right now we run our programs Monday through Wednesday. The only day that we don't have any programs running is on Thursday. Friday generally are a recap of the week for us," Eunice says.

"Thursday seem to be wide open. How does Thursday sound to you?" Donnell then asks. "If it doesn't work, we can figure something out on another day."

"Oh no, Thursdays will be just fine for me. Great, how about this coming Thursday at 7pm?" Eunice asks.

"Sounds good to me," Donnell replies.

"Ok, see you then," Eunice says.

Thursday arrives, and Donnell is both anxious and a little nervous about his first visit to Ohallowbee. He pulls into the parking lot and gets out of his vehicle for a second, but quickly re-enters his car to say a short prayer. Meanwhile, inside of Ohallowbee, the boys have no idea that he's there. They are busy watching T.V., playing cards, and working out.

Their activities are interrupted when an announcement from the operator's room comes across the intercom. *"ALL DETAINEES REPORT TO THE DAY ROOM, I REPEAT... REPORT TO THE DAY ROOM IMMEDIATELY."*

After a few grunts and complaints, they all put on their jumpsuits. The officers on duty order them to line up single file and then to proceed to the day room. One by one they enter the day room with hands folded behind their backs and are seated. The look on their faces says it all. They are surprised, but more so excited to see who the person standing in front of them is. Ms. Eaton, sporting a smile on her face asks, "Do any of you recognize this man?"

It appears nobody wants to be the first one to raise their hand out of the fear of looking stupid in case they don't remember Donnell's name. A hand goes up. It belongs to none other than Brandon Bright, whom Donnell had a huge impact on in the courtroom, "Yeah, I remember him. That's Ol' boy from court that talked to us, Mr. White or something like that."

"Nice memory, Brandon. I see that somebody was paying attention that day in the courtroom," Ms. Eaton says. "Well, I won't hold you up any longer than I already have Mr. White, they are all yours."

"Thank you! Ms. Eaton," Donnell says, "And I appreciate the opportunity that you and Mr. Jones have given me to work with the boys here at Ohallowbee. Before I start, I'd like to come out to shake each one of your hands and get your names individually if ya'll don't mind? That way we can all get on a personal level and I can treat you as family."

Donnell makes his rounds and after shaking the hand of the last boy, he does something totally unexpected. He pulls up a chair in the middle of all of them and asks them to form a circle around him. Then, he says, "The reason why I've asked you guys to form this circle around me is because I want to be the one in the middle so no matter which way I turn, one of you guys will be there.

I also want to show you guys, rather than talk, that I'm here for the long haul, and I'll be where you can all see me. This is our *Inner Circle,* and I'd rather already be inside of it than outside of it seeking to get in. I know what it's like being locked up. You have no ownership of anything. Not even

The Compass of a Conscience

your own lives. No one can enter our circle, but us, unless one of you guys or myself bring them in. I've elected to be the man in the middle, where any of you guys can come and talk to me anytime you like."

"Are you guys cool with that?"

He turns around and looks at the boys' eyes as their heads nod yes. Unsatisfied with their replies Donnell says, "You know where I'm from and how I was raised is that a man shouldn't be afraid to open up his mouth and speak to another man like a man. So, since I'm a man who's talking to young men, I need to hear your voices.

He repeats, "Am I a part of this circle or not?"

The reply is unlike any that the staff of Ohallowbee has ever witnessed before. A thunderous sound of *"Yes Sir,"* saturates the room, so much so that the staff begins whispering to one another in amazement. A few of them leave and bring back more personnel until eventually the director himself, Mr. Jones, eases in for the duration of the session. They all are impressed with Mr. White's ability to capture the attention of all the detainees.

It is as if he has them eating from the palms of his hand, but Ms. Eaton savors the moment within herself. She has been recording the entire session on her cell phone the whole time.

Donnell extends both arms with the palms of each hand facing the group and asks them, "Do you guys know what these are and what they have done?"

With strange looks on their faces, nobody in the group wants to say anything.

"Allow me to tell you," Donnell says.

"These are hands that you're looking at. These hands have destroyed people and controlled communities for a very long time. These hands have made and spent millions! In times past these hands were used for destruction, but now they're used for rebuilding. You really can't see the effects of what you're doing while you're doing it, until the reality of what you've done sets in.

In most cases, it's too late and the damage is already done. That's why I've decided not to make it a priority to give you guys the details about the who, what, where & when. I'd rather discuss "*The Why,*" right now. We'll have plenty of time for discussion about the other ones later.

Let's be clear on one thing. I didn't come in here to fake the funk with you fellas. The imprisonment you guys are currently serving is cake walk in comparison to prison. I don't know how you are being treated but I'll say this, I hope that this place and the staff here is making your lives a living hell! You want to know why? It's because I don't want you

The Compass of a Conscience

getting comfortable coming to a place like this, because this isn't life!

By God's design you could never live in a place where your sole purpose is only to exist. Which brings me to my next point. It's nobody's fault but your own that you are in the situation you're in. It's not mom or dad's fault and for the record, neither is the officer who arrested you at fault. I can tell you right now that the hardest thing that you'll ever have to face is yourself. You've got to acknowledge a need for change at this point in your lives. You can't change what you don't recognize to be a problem. *"The Why"* is so important because it helps us to identify the problem.

You were all present in the courtroom to witness my release from prison. I am fully aware that I'm a free man, but as you can see, I came back to jail. I came back because I care about what happens to you guys and I want to make a difference in your lives. Every time I come here to see y'all it reminds me that I'm only one mistake away from being in the same position. My decision to be here today had nothing to do with what I wanted at all. I needed to be here with you guys because my story plus your story equals *"Our Story."* In this place, you got nothing but time on your hands. Time to reflect, time to listen, and time to change."

Donnell holds back no punches and talks to the boys as though they were all men that day. After an entire hour of lecturing and answering questions from the boys and various staff personnel, Donnell closes, to everyone's surprise, by presenting a question to the boys.

"Who tells you what to do?"

Some of the boys say "Nobody," while others mutter "Me," but no one is willing to step into the spotlight and answer the question confidently. Donnell talks to Brandon directly then, "Allow me to pick on you for a second, if you don't mind. If I were to tell you to do something that might get you killed, would you do it?"

"No," Brandon says.

"Why not?" Donnell asks.

"Because I'm not gonna allow anybody to talk me into doing something that can get me killed," Brandon says. "Besides, I don't wanna die either so I'm gonna do what's best for me."

Donnell replies, "So, would it be correct to say that you tell yourself what to do? Meaning that you only do what you tell yourself to do and there's no one other than yourself who can make you do anything you don't want to do?"

"Am I correct," Brandon?

"Pretty much yeah," Brandon replies.

"Ok," Brandon Donnell says. "Since we've established that you tell yourself what to do, and you answer only to yourself, I want you to think back over your life and answer this question. Who was it that told you what to do when you did what you did to get yourself locked up?"

"Me, I guess," Brandon says.

"You got that right, my man!" Donnell replies. "The moral of the story is that we can either be the biggest asset for ourselves or the greatest threat to ourselves. So, be mindful of what *YOU* tell *YOURSELF* to do. Comprende?"

The partial smile that rested on the faces of all the boys indicated that the light bulb in their minds had just come on.

"I want to leave you all with something to ponder on," Donnell says.

"Change doesn't come cheap! It's an investment that will cost you something. My challenge to you guys is simple, if not now then, when? If I can change, anybody can change!"

"Well, that's my time for today," Donnell tells them. "I would like to thank the Ohallowbee Detention Center for allowing me to come in and become a mentor to you guys.

I appreciate the efforts of the entire staff here, and Ms. Eaton for having the vision to ask me to volunteer. Special thanks to Mr. Jones for allowing it to happen.

My final thanks are to you guys, for allowing me to adopt you as my little brothers. You guys are why I'm here. If

I can help one, just one of you guys, change your lives for the better my work will be meaningful. It's been such a blessing, and a lot of fun hanging out with you all this evening.

Don't think that this is the last you've seen of me either, because I'll be coming once a week on Thursdays until I'm told that I can't come anymore. You might as well as get used to seeing this ugly face around here."

The boys chuckle and giggle. It is from that moment on that Brandon knows deep down that there is something special about Mr. White, and he begins to develop a bond with him.

Chapter 14
The Riot

"Lights out!" blares across the P.A system at Ohallowbee Detention Center for boys. It's 11:00 pm on a Friday night, and the boys are restless and getting a little rowdy. Chief Officer Bernard Williams begins to make his rounds ordering the boys to their bunks.

The boys start complaining and simultaneously ask Officer Williams, "Ah, c'mon Officer Williams! Let us ride out for at least another hour until midnight."

"You guys already know what time it is with me, and how I get down," states Officer Williams. "I suggest you all return to your bunks before I start taking away privileges around here."

One by one, voices start mumbling... *Faggot, Sissy, Punk mother...*

"You girls got something ya'll want to say to me?" Asks Officer Williams while approaching the group."

No one responds but the cold stares in their eyes say it all.

"Yeah! That's what I thought," Officer Williams says. "Now stand by them bunks while I complete my headcount to make sure none of you punks have escaped."

As he passes each detainee staring them up and down, you couldn't help but notice the sinister grin upon his face. He knew that he had the authority to make their lives miserable and he loved every minute of it.

Later that night. A few hours past midnight, an Officer in Distress (OID) siren goes off in Ohallowbee's West Unit Sector. The distress call was triggered from the panic button attached to Officer Williams' collar. Mandatory policy of Ohallowbee requires all staff to wear a panic button during their shift for their safety.

Once a panic button is pressed, all staff must immediately stop what they're doing and report to the location of the issue. As they all arrive, the scene is reminiscent of a riot in a prison movie. Toilet paper hurdled, hanging from the ceiling, and even stuck to the walls. Mattresses are scattered across the floor and bunks overturned. In the aftermath, lies the beaten body of a 16-year-old boy, who barely has a pulse. The boy's identity is confirmed as Brandon Bright.

Staff members fear the worst as he lays unconscious and motionless on the cold concrete floor. The bruises and marks around his neck prompt staff members to perform CPR while

The Compass of a Conscience

waiting for the arrival of the paramedics. By the time the paramedics arrive, the atmosphere and morale of the detainees and staff is very somber. Brandon's nearly lifeless body is transported to St. Peter Memorial Hospital.

Upon arriving, Brandon is taken to the critical care unit where doctors race to examine his injuries.

He is given a CAT scan and X-ray to decide what procedures are necessary to save his life. The results of the X-ray showed some unusual swelling and fluid around Brandon's spinal cord. The doctors explained their findings to representatives of Ohallowbee accompanying Brandon to the hospital. Emergency surgery is needed. The doctors waste no time to operate.

The surgery lasts for hours and the physicians finally emerge saying, "Brandon is in a stable condition."

They tell the representatives that due to the aggressive nature of the strangulation he received, his spinal cord suffered severe trauma. He's been placed in a medically induced coma. The doctors go on to say that, their purpose is to prevent further trauma that could possibly result in him having a stroke.

"We've done everything that we can possibly do for him. It's all up to him now. At this point we cannot say if it will be a permanent condition for him, but if he pulls through this, he will most likely be paralyzed."

Chapter 15
Power Struggle

Several days have passed since the uproar at Ohallowbee and Donnell returns for his regular scheduled Thursday evening session with the boys. As he clears security, he can't help but notice how quiet the place is. He makes his way into the day room where he's accustomed to seeing the boys and no one is in there.

Mr. Jones, the center's director, signals him to come over to his office, and Donnell starts walking in that direction. Once inside of his office, Mr. Jones wastes no time breaking the news to Mr. White.

"I'm sorry to inform you that over the past weekend we had a riot. During the incident, unfortunately, one of our detainees was gravely injured. It was the first riot I've ever experienced, in my thirty plus years in the criminal justice system. I've supervised jails and road prisons before and nothing like this has ever happened under my watchful eye."

"Oh wow! So, do you have any idea of what started it?" Donnell asks.

"Due to federal restrictions and state regulations, I am not at liberty to discuss the details with you," Mr. Jones replies.

The Compass of a Conscience

"What I called you into my office for is to inform you of who got hurt. It was Brandon Bright. I know that the two of you had formed a bond, and were starting to connect with one another."

"Brandon wasn't the only person in the group that I was trying to reach," Donnell says. "It is my desire to form a formidable bond with every detainee here at Ohaollowbee. Brandon just so happened to be the kind of kid who is passionate about life and wears his heart on his sleeve. This really bums me out because that kid really wanted to change. I'd like to speak to his parents or whomever I need to speak with about visiting him," Donnell says.

"Again, due to federal restrictions and state regulations, I am not permitted to divulge such information to unauthorized personnel, repeats Mr. Jones. Just so you know, Brandon has no family that we are aware of. That's about all I can say to you about the matter. You might want to talk to our nurse on-duty Mrs. Adams. Maybe she can help you, but you did not hear that from me. Are we clear about what I just said?"

"Yes, crystal clear Mr. Jones," Donnell says. "I'll go and speak with her now. "Thanks," Donnell replies.

As he is leaving Mr. Jones office, Donnell runs into Officer Bernard Williams in the hallway.

"Good afternoon Mr. White," Officer Williams says.

"Hello there, Officer Williams. How's it going?" Donnell asks.

"Considering the recent events, which I'm sure Mr. Jones has just informed you of, everything is just starting to get back to normal around here," Officer Williams says.

"I understand. I just really hate that Brandon got hurt, or any kid in the program, for that matter," Donnell states.

"You see, that's just it," said Officer Williams. "I believe in karma. I hate that the kid got hurt too, but I think he brought it on himself. Kids like Brandon are awful detainees and make our jobs as correctional officers a living hell. They abuse the system because they know we are restricted in the amount of force we can use on them. Little criminals."

Donnell responds, "Criminals? Are you kidding me???"

"I guess I don't have to question my reason for being here because now I see that it is for a divine purpose. What they need is to be treated like they are human beings, especially from the people who are in the position that you're in. Yes! I said humans because that's who they are first, not criminals. I can imagine how you talk to them every day after having this conversation with you."

"Now, you just hold up there, convict, ex-convict, or whatever you go by," Officer Williams says. "You seem to have a misunderstanding of your role here, buddy! Let's not forget who has the authority around here. When it comes to criminal justice, I'm the one with the degree and the experience not you.

At best, you're just a poster boy of what not to be when they grow up. I get paid good money for working here. You're just a volunteer. Remember that!"

"You know what Officer Williams? You sound weak and pathetic to me. If what you do is so awesome then why is there a need for my presence around here?" Donnell asks. You might think you're the authority, but real authority you possess not. That's because you lack meaningful character. If you can name an instance where you have tried to make a difference in someone else life other than your own I'll shut my mouth and agree with everything you just said but we both know that you can't, right? Unlike those boys, you can't belittle me and kill my morale. No sir, I know your type. You are a bad actor and a bully! In fact, you are the quintessential of what you've been calling these boys. A PUNK! As far as we are concerned, I'll stay out of your way and I ask that you do the same for me," Donnell says.

Mrs. Adams approaches them then, and says, "Good evening gentlemen."

They both greet her at the same time.

"Hello Mrs. Adams."

"Hi there, Mrs. Adams."

"I hope I didn't interrupt anything. Whatever conversation you two seemed to be having, you cut it short rather abruptly when you guys saw me approaching..."

Simultaneously, Donnell and Officer Williams says, "No, no, not at all."

"Mr. White and I were just discussing how to improve the officer/detainee relations around here. Isn't that right, Mr. White?" Officer William asks.

With a look of disgust on his face at the hypocrisy of Officer Williams' statement, Donnell reluctantly agrees and says "Yeah." Then he adds, "I do have something to discuss with you, Mrs. Adams, if you have a minute?" Donnell asks.

"I sure do, Mr. White. We can talk privately in my office," Mrs. Adams replies.

"Thanks," Donnell says. Give me a second and I'll be in to talk to you.

"Ok, see you in a bit," Mrs. Adams replies.

Out of the fear of not knowing what Donnell wants to discuss with Mrs. Adams, Officer Williams attempts to recant his previous assertions. He extends his hand out in hopes that Donnell will do the same and states, "Look, Mr. White, we both probably said a little too much to each other, but I believe that we can work together and be professionals here."

The expression on Donnell's face says it all. He stands there staring Officer Williams straight in the eyes before walking away without a single word.

Chapter 16
Eyes Wide Open

Brandon lies in bed motionless, without the usual sound of the life support machine he's been on. He has made a lot of progress and is now breathing on his own. Slowly his eyes begin to twitch and gradually open. Heavily sedated, he struggles to bring into focus the blurred silhouette of the person in the room. Once his vision is completely restored, he stares with perplexity at his surroundings and wonders why he is in a hospital and why is this individual there also. With a very weak tone in his voice he utters, "What's up?"

The individual approaches saying, "Bran-Bran the man... Do you recognize who I am?" He asks.

"Yeah... What's going on Mr. White? And why am I in a hospital?"

"That's a long story I'm hoping you can shed some light on it when you get well. You don't remember anything at all?" Donnell asks.

"I remember that punk motherf--ker on my back choking me," Brandon says.

"What are you talking about? Who attacked you?" Donnell asks.

The Compass of a Conscience

"Nothing, nobody. Nevermind Mr. White," Brandon says.

"Ok, no problem," Donnell says, but if you decide later that you want to talk about it, I'm here. There's something you should know but I think it's best the doctors talk with you about it."

"What do you mean? Brandon asks. It ain't no doctors in here. All I see is us two."

"Ok, Brandon," Donnell replies, "but before I tell you anything, I need you to do me a huge favor first."

"What?" Brandon asks.

"Lift up your legs so that I can put socks on your feet," Donnell says.

Brandon tries fervently to move his legs but to no avail. He looks then at Donnell and asks desperately, "Why can't I feel nothing in my legs?" With tears forming in his eyes he softly whispers, "Help me, Mr. White, you gotta do something, please?"

His plea proves to be more than Donnell can handle. He turns away from Brandon to wipe away tears and gather himself together before trying to calm Brandon down. A grief-stricken Donnell says, "Brandon, I'm sorry but you are—"

He's interrupted by Brandon crying, and saying, "I rather be dead than to live like this. If I gotta live like this, I won't be living long. I rather kill myself, I can't take it!"

Donnell tells Brandon that he'll be right back, and leaves the room. He goes to the parking lot, enters his vehicle and cry harder than Brandon did. He remains there until he feels strong enough to face Brandon without breaking down again. He knows that Brandon will need someone strong in his corner, helping him cope with his situation. He returns to Brandon's room only to see a disheartening site. There on the bed sat this young confused kid punching himself in the legs.

At that moment, Donnell knows he's got a decision to make concerning his involvement in Brandon's recovery. He knows that his response to what he is seeing now is critical. The way he handles this situation will determine his role in Brandon's recovery. But seeing Brandon have a complete meltdown triggered memories of a fatal event from Donnell's past. A tragedy that he thought that he had long since accepted and gotten over.

There had been a period of his life when he had felt the exact same feeling of hopelessness that Brandon was now feeling. This event came at a time in his life when he was old enough to understand the ordeal but was way too young to process it. He had witnessed the shooting death of his childhood friend Anton. Caught up in the heavy influx of memories, he began to enter a trance-like state of mind and rehashed it all over again.

It was 1987, and he was 12-years-old. His friend Anton was tall and skinny with a 2-year age difference at 14. Anton's face was riddled with pimples and he had a chipped front tooth. He and Donnell had been friends since they were toddlers.

They were inseparable and at no time could you see one without the other.

The neighborhood that they grew up in wasn't the ideal environment for a kid to be brought up in. Nonetheless, it was their reality. The boys saw everything, heard way too much, and were exposed to things that most adults haven't been exposed to. He remembered having to leave his house for school around 5am at the dawning of daylight but still dark outside.

On the way to the bus stop he'd sometimes see a prostitute performing oral sex on someone in an alleyway. A few times he'd just stand there watching them go at it until he was spotted. One time, a guy cursed and threatened him by saying things like, "What the hell you are you looking at, you lil muthaf--ka!?! You better get your little curious a-- on down there to your bus stop or wherever the f--k you were going!"

Sex and the threat of physical violence wasn't the only hazard he had been exposed to. Also, on his route to the bus stop, he'd see used and discarded syringes dropped on the sidewalks by heroin addicts. Every so often for kicks, Donnell or one of his friends would pick one up and chase each other around. He even remembered old man Mr. Ed shooting his gun in the air a few times whenever he caught them jumping his gate, and raiding his plum tree. Old man Ed's favorite line was, "If I catch one of you little bastards in my yard as God be my witness imma kill one of ya thieving a--es!"

These thoughts raced through Donnell's mind marginally; however, Brandon's situation triggered the more critical thoughts about Anton's death. Anton was an innocent bystander that received the fate intended for JoJo and his cousin Flooty.

One of Anton's biggest problems during his short life was that he wanted to grow up way too fast. He'd always try to run with boys much older than he and Donnell were. This would ultimately cost him his life. His first warning came when JoJo, who was 17-years-old, fired shots to a group in which Anton was among. Luckily nobody was injured that day. That alone should've made him rethink his choice of friends and the circles that he ran in, but it didn't. Anton had a knack of being in the wrong place at the wrong time.

The day of his death proved to make that assertion real to Donnell, as he remembered what he had experienced that day. JoJo was well known for his trigger-happy activities and, quite naturally, had a lot of enemies. In a twist of fate, Anton was hanging out with JoJo and Flooty the day he was killed.

Anton and Donnell had many conversations about not liking JoJo and Flooty. That's why it didn't sit well with Donnell when he saw Anton, JoJo, and Flooty hanging around together the day Anton died. Why Anton was hanging around them perplexed and infuriated him all at the same time. So, he decided not to approach Anton and turned around heading in the opposite direction. It was a decision he'd live to regret for many years to come.

While he was walking away, Donnell noticed a blue Oldsmobile with a group of guys in it. At first glance, nothing about the car or the guys alarmed him. It wasn't until he passed the vehicle and overheard the conversation inside that he knew something bad was about to go down. He walked a little further before it dawned on him that Anton's life was in danger. At that point, all he could do was think about going back to warn Anton, but time waits for no one. By the time he returned to where the vehicle had once been parked, Donnell noticed that it was now gone and, before he knew it, gunshots erupted.

Growing up in the streets, you learn to do certain things by nature, and upon hearing those gunshots, Donnell's natural response was to hit the ground until the coast was clear. When the gunshots ceased, two more single shots came from the blue Oldsmobile as it sped off. Donnell noticed JoJo crawling on the sidewalk, injured from a gunshot wound. Flooty, his cousin, peeped his head around the building, and when he noticed that the coast was clear, he took off running to safety. Unable to move, Donnell laid there on the ground expecting to see Anton's face emerge next. He never did.

The screams and cries of everybody running to the scene said it all. His worst fear had come true and he knew that Anton had been shot. What he didn't know was that it was fatal. The crowd that gathered grew as the cops struggled to secure the area. People were crying and asking Donnell if he was ok but their voices all sounded robotic and slurred. He was a kid who was completely devastated and in shock about what he had just witnessed.

Donnell took Anton's death hard and blamed himself for not warning Anton about the danger his life was in. Somehow, someway he felt as though if he had done so Anton would still be alive today. What made things worse was finding out later that the real target had been JoJo for something he had done to those guys.

Anton had been in the wrong place at the wrong time for the last time. JoJo, on the other hand, had lived to continue doing the same stuff that ultimately had cost Anton his life.

The Compass of a Conscience

Life can be so unfair and cruel, Donnell thought to himself comparing the outcome of both Anton and Brandon's lives.

Brandon interrupts Donnell's thoughts by waving his hands and saying, "Hey, can you hear me, Mr. White?"

Donnell snaps out of his deep thoughts and says, "Yeah, I hear you... what is it, Brandon? Are you good?"

"I ain't gonna lie to you, Mr. White. This is some bulls--t. I just feel like my life is over and I don't wanna live like this, because this ain't living at all."

"This is not a death sentence unless you make it one, Brandon. Life has taught me that it is not until we are lying flat on our backs that we even realize that there's a need for us to get up. A slam dunk doesn't count as a dunk unless it fully clears the net. Meaning, nothing that happens in our lives is final. Nope. Not until we accept it as such. Yes, your life as you knew it before will be altered, but consider this: There are billions of souls that would trade places with you in a heartbeat just to have another chance to be among the living and breathing. To hear things like you hear and to see the things you see, and to feel what you are feeling right now, Brandon.

They can't, and they never will again but this is not the end for you. I believe that Christ Jesus is using this situation in your life to do something miraculous through you and in you. Do you remember when we first met in the courtroom that day and you were saying that all you had in this life was yourself to depend on?"

"Yes, sir. I remember that day," said Brandon.

"If I recall it right, I believe that I flat out told you that everybody is going to need someone at some point in their life. Do you remember us discussing that as well?" Donnell asks.

"Yep! But I gotta ask you a question," Mr. White.

"Go ahead."

"Are you always this deep? Geesh!"

[They both laugh.]

"I'm thankful that you can find some peace and laughter right now because I believe that God has put us into each other's lives for a reason. I, for one, plan on fulfilling my purpose in your life, Brandon and as I mentioned to you guys at our first session, get used to seeing this ugly face because I'm not going anywhere anytime soon."

Somehow, hearing Donnell say those words brings a calm and peace to Brandon's mind.

"Well Brandon, it's getting late and I need to get home so that I can eat and shower. I got to be ready for work tomorrow, but I'll be back to see you afterwards."

"Are you good with that Brandon?"

"I'm good, Mr. White."

"Ok then. Be easy Brandon."

"I will. You too, Mr. White."

Donnell's drive back home is far from ordinary and it becomes a bit of a challenge to reach his destination on time due to missed exits and turns. His mind is heavily consumed with questions about what went down at the detention center with Brandon. It bothers him so severely that it impacts his ability to focus on driving. From that moment on, he wants to get to the bottom of how something like this could happen in a relatively controlled facility.

Chapter 17
Uninvited Guest

The next morning, Brandon gets a visit from some very interesting and strangely behaving visitors.

"Good morning to you, young man."

Stretching and yawning, Brandon says, "What's up?"

"I'm Brother Al and this here is my brother in the Lord, Tommy. What is your name young man?"

"Brandon. What do you guys want?"

"Good question, Brandon. We are messengers sent on behalf of The Heavenly Language Ministries. We are here to impart the gift of Tongues to you and teach you how to speak in Tongues. I have a quick question for you, Brandon. Are you saved, son?"

"Nope," Brandon replies.

"Well, we promise not to take up too much of your time because we want to spread the gift to all the sick in this medical facility. If you don't mind we'd like to say a prayer with you?"

"Alright. I mean…Yeah, okay I guess."

"Now, as we pray, the spirit will come upon you and shall overtake you and cause you to speak in unknown tongues, but don't be afraid or dismayed. This is your calling."

"Huh?" Said Brandon.

"What you talking about, man? I don't know if I'm cool with..."

Before Brandon could finish his sentence, Brother Al began praying.

"*Lord, we rebuke that spirit of rebellion and doubt and we cast it back to the pits of hell from whence it came. Loosen his tongue, lord, so that he may speak utterances unknown to man. Ah-la-la-Hah, Ooh-Ah-Cah, Ta-ta-Too, Ta-ta-Too...*"

After putting up with their gyrating for a moment or two, Brandon has seen and heard enough, and decides to end the charade.

"Sir, could you... Sir, HEY SIR!" Yells Brandon.

"Is there a problem, Brandon? There's nothing to be afraid of, son."

"Look man, I don't know what kind of language y'all trying to get me to speak but let me ask you guys something."

"Sure thing. You can ask us anything you want to, Brandon."

"Do y'all curse?"

"Not at all, Brandon. Why would you ask us something like that, son?"

"Because I do. And if you two don't get the hell outta here with that all that crazy a—sh-t that y'all doing I'm about to curse y'all clean the f--k out!"

"Have it your way, son, but we will mark this day as the day that the heathen has lifted up his heel against the messengers of the highest. We will henceforth return no more. We shall shake the dust off our feet as a witness that it may be accounted a curse upon you. We pray for your lost soul son."

"Oh no, sir! Don't you pray for me or anybody else in this hospital for that reason. That's the kind of prayer that you need to keep all for yourself and for your comrade that you brought along with you there. Thanks, but no thanks! I'm good!"

Chapter 18
Date with Destiny

The temperature outside reaches somewhere around 90 degrees. Donnell is at work on his construction job, sweating profusely and occasionally checking his watch in anticipation of lunch time. He notices a missed call, followed by a voicemail icon displayed across the screen of his cell phone. During his lunch break he checks his voicemail first.

"Hello, this message is for Donnell White. My name is Oleta Oukinuwin. I am a social worker and counselor here at the Base for Boys. I received your contact info from a colleague of mine, Ms. Eunice Eaton. I was wondering if it might be possible to meet and discuss the possibilities of you working with our program in the future. If you could please return my call at 850-207-4600 ext. 102, I'd greatly appreciate it. Have a nice day and I look forward to hearing from you."

Donnell wastes no time returning the call. Ms. Oukinuwin answers and says, "Hello, you've reached the Base for Boys. This is Oleta speaking. How may I assist you?"

"Hi there. Is this Ms. Oleta Oukinuwin?" Donnell asks.

"The one and only, she replies, and to who do I have the pleasure of speaking with?"

"My name is Donnell White. You left me a voicemail message a little while ago."

"Yes, yes, I did. Thanks for returning my call, Sir. I had the privilege of viewing the video of your first visit to the Ohallowbee Detention Center. It was amazing! I also heard about the powerful speech you gave the boys in the courtroom as well. I hope there's still enough of you to go around? We desperately need someone like yourself who can share your experiences with our group of boys."

"I'm all for it, Ms. Oukinuwin. Just tell me when and where. I have a few activities on my plate right now, but I'm sure that we can work something out."

"Oh, absolutely, Mr. White. I don't want to complicate your time or schedule at all. When can we meet? My office is located here at the Base for Boys. If you prefer a different locale I can accommodate you on that with ease."

"Ok, Ms. Oukinuwin. I'm not working tomorrow so I can meet you at your office sometime in the morning."

"Awesome! I'm in meetings from 7:30-8:45am tomorrow. How does 9am sound? Ms. Oukinuwin asks."

"Sounds good to me," Donnell replies.

Ms. Oukinuwin says, Great! "I look forward to seeing you then. In the meantime, I'll send a text to your phone with directions on how to get here."

"Likewise, and I'll keep an eye out for your text. Enjoy the rest of your day."

"Thanks Mr. White. You do the same."

The next day, Donnell shows up around 8:30am and he waits another forty-five minutes in the lobby for Ms. Oukinuwin. At 9:15am, a woman emerges that, in Donnell's opinion, is the most beautiful woman he's ever seen.

She is about 5ft. 6 inches, athletically shaped with short wavy styled hair. She has smooth olive skin that is rich in melanin. The size and shape of her eyes is unlike any on a woman's face that Donnell had ever seen.

She introduces herself, shakes his hand and escorts him to her office. Meanwhile, she also introduces him to various faculty along the way. Once they reach her office and are alone inside, the vibe between them was sort of a love at first sight experience. Their apparent attraction to one another and their chemistry with each other was undeniable.

Turning the charm on, Donnell says, "Wow! You're so beautiful it baffles me. I don't usually speak in unlearned languages but, *Comment allez-vous?* Or should I be saying, *Hola,¿cómo estás?* I'm sure you're getting the point I'm trying to make here? I'm not trying to appear unprofessional but when I first heard your name I thought I'd be meeting a middle-aged woman. One who perhaps had a few facial whiskers... but you're gorgeous! I hope that you don't get offended by my asking you this, but are you bi-racial?"

"I am bi-racial, and I'm not offended by your question at all. I get asked that all the time. My mother is Black, and my father is Asian," Ms. Oukinuwin replies. "My first name came from my deceased grandmother Oleta, and of course you should have guessed by now where my last name comes from. Thank you for the compliment and I see that you are a pretty humorous guy who's internalized speaking basic greetings in French and Spanish. I love French. I speak it as my second language, you know?"

"Oh really?" Donnell asks. "Well, in that case, *Oooh la la Wee Wee.*"

Ms. Oukinuwin bursts into laughter and says, "You're so silly. Your personality is so cool." She wastes no time to say, "*Votre francais est terrible et assez elementaire.*" That's to say, *Your French is terrible and quite elementary.* "Your approach is creative and by the way you're quite easy on the eyes yourself there, Mister. I have something to ask you and I apologize in advance if it catches you off guard, but this was just put in my lap this morning. The board wanted me to ask you if you'd be interested in speaking to the group this morning?"

"Sure! I'd love to," Donnell replies.

"*REALLY?*" Ms. Oukinuwin asks. "I must warn you before you go in and meet with the group that these boys are street-wise and can be extremely rude. Hopefully you can hold your own in this kind of environment because they are a handful."

"I come from that element, Ms. Oukinuwin. I'm not afraid of them and I have pretty-thick skin you know. I'm not here to try and impress them. My mission is to show them that there is a better way that they more than likely haven't given any real thought to. In the streets, there is an old saying that "Real Recognizes Real."

"My task is to be myself and that's about as real as it gets. Shall we? he asks finally, as he motions with the sway of this hand and bows partially."

Ms. Oukinuwin's enthusiasm is reflected in the huge smile she gives Donnell. So much so that if one were to be that meticulous, he or she could count every tooth in her mouth at that moment. As accustomed, Donnell unfolded details about experiences in his life to a large group integrated of both staff and detainees, and he ends with some words of wisdom.

There's a Q and A segment that requires every person in the room to participate. They had to reflect on and think about reasonable solutions when responding to situational occurrences. The outcome was unlike anything that anyone there had expected, and an overwhelming number of requests to speak personally with Donnell come from the boys and staff alike. Initially, what was supposed to be a meeting, becomes a turning point experience in the lives of some that day.

"Oh my God! I am speechless right now, Ms. Oukinuwin exclaims. I was impressed when I saw the recording of you at Ohallowbee but to experience it live right before my very eyes is mind blowing.

I've never seen this group respect or respond in a manner like that to any guest speaker that has ever walked through these doors. The morale between staff and the boys have never been this way before. Please tell me how can we get you to return?"

"Well, for starters, you can allow me to take you out for dinner."

"Hmmm... I don't know about that," Mr. White.

"Maybe I'm fishing in a dry pond with this statement," Ms. Oukinuwin, "but your response leaves me to believe that there might be a possibility in there somewhere?"

"Ummm... there could be a slight possibility," Mr. White.

"Look," Says Donnell. "I'm aware that this may not be the time or the place. You have my number. Call me anytime."

"I'll take that into consideration," Mr. White. Replies Ms. Oukinuwin, and once again, "thank you for coming out and agreeing on such short notice to speak to the group."

"My pleasure and I look forward to returning again. Until then, take care and remain beautiful," Ms. Oukinuwin.

"Aww... that's so sweet of you," Mr. White. "I hope that you continue to spread your contagious positivity everywhere you go, sir."

Later that day as Donnell is out and about, his phone rings. He is pleasantly surprised to hear the voice of the person on the other end. That voice is that of none other than Ms. Oukinuwin herself.

"Hello," Mr. White. "Did I catch you at a bad time?

"Ah, c'mon," Ms. Oukinuwin. "As pretty as you are, you don't have to be fishing around. You've had me hooked on you since we met this morning."

"You are so funny and have such a likable personality," Mr. White. "Be careful there, smooth talker, us ladies can get used to that kind of treatment."

"Hey, it is what it is with me, sweetheart. I say what I mean, and I meant what I just said. In that order."

"The reason for my call is to see if your offer for dinner is still standing? I have some ideas that I'd like to throw your way."

"Sure. When do you want to meet?"

"That is entirely up to you," Sir. "When will you be available?"

"Are you serious," Ms. Oukinuwin? "Ok, so you and I gotta go back through the steps again huh? As far you go access to me is always granted. Unrestricted and 24/7. How does that sound to you?"

Ms. Oukinuwin laughs and says: "You are too much… How does 7 or 8pm tonight sound?"

"Sounds good to me."

"Ok, see you then. And don't worry about where we'll meet. I have a place in mind and I'll send directions to you shortly."

"I'll be right here waiting."

A few hours had gone by and Donnell still hasn't received the text of the location from Ms. Oukinuwin. Before he can begin to wonder about it, his phone text message alert sounds with the name of the restaurant and directions of how to get there.

Donnell arrives minutes before Ms. Oukinuwin does and decides to have a seat at the bar. He wants to be close enough to the entrance to personally greet her as she walks in. A few minutes later, Ms. Oukinuwin arrives.

When Donnell sees her, he loses all composure and freezes in awe of the person he is looking at.

"Hello," Sir. "It's good to see you for the second time today."

Donnell replies with a very seductive "Hellooo," Ms. Oukinuwin, as he gently raises her hand to kiss it softly.

In a joking manner, Ms. Oukinuwin sarcastically says: "Oh, earlier today you were Romeo. Romeo, wherefore art thou? You mean to tell me that all a girl gets is a kiss on the hand now? Should I or shouldn't I be offended? You tell me," Sir?

"Now hold up! W-w-wait a second!! When I saw you enter through that door my mind did exactly what eyes and body did, and that was "FAIL TO PROPERLY ADJUST!"

"Collectively the three of us are still trying to get it together after seeing you. Don't you worry about it though, I think we're all on the same page now."

"Now, that's the guy I came expecting to see."

The two of them embrace in a modest hug before being interrupted by the hostess asking: "Where do you guys want to be seated?"

They agree on a booth and are seated.

Once the conversation begins, it never seems to end. What Ms. Oukinuwin's focus seems to be centered on is Donnell's direction in life now. She sees something in him that he apparently doesn't see for himself at the time.

He tells her his entire life story. He also tells her about his desire to form a non-profit organization. One that is specifically designed to influence, educate, and eradicate the hopelessness of so many youths in the community. He also mentions to her his current situation with Brandon.

After Donnell somewhat bares his soul to her, she feels comfortable enough to reveal a few personal details about her life to him. She tells him that she too has had family members and friends who have been on the opposite side of the law as well.

"You are so passionate and determined to make something better out of yourself, and everyone who comes into contact with you," Mr. White.

"Please Oleta, call me Donnell, replied Mr.White."

"As you wish," she replied.

What I am saying is, that's so inspirational to me. I've come across so many so-called victims blaming everything on everybody for their circumstances. It's so disappointing but then a rarity like yourself comes along and gives me so much hope.

Regardless of the mistakes that you've made I see a man who is a born leader. You possess a gift to inspire individuals whom some people feel are beyond encouraging. I can't tell you how many of my colleagues don't believe that someone of your background can change, but you're proving them wrong. It's amazing to me how parallel our goals and desires are. If you like I can help you make your desire to start a non-profit more of a reality. I can help you get your 501c3 status, write grant proposals and secure funding."

The outcome resulting from that meeting was such that neither Donnell nor Ms. Oukinuwin could have ever imagined then nor in the time to come. Many things materialized from that night. A beautiful relationship ensued, both personally and professionally, -- the idea of the "Boys

Will Be Boys Foundation *(BWBBF)"* was given birth that night.

Chapter 19
Checking in

It is Thursday evening, and it's Donnell's first visit since the incident involving Brandon being hospitalized. The boys are excited and can't wait to see him. As soon he enters the room, he's bombarded with questions about Brandon. A few of them seek a private moment with Donnell but Officer Williams forbids any such communication.

Before he begins, Donnell passes around a black binder that has clear pocket sleeves bearing pictures. Inside are pictures of himself showing off various possessions that he used to own as a drug dealer. Row upon row and page after page displayed cars, women, and jewels. There's one though in particular, that repeatedly received *Ooh's* and *Ah's* when everyone sees it.

It is a picture in which Donnell is sitting at a dining room table with a half million dollars cash laid out before him. It's something the boys and the staff have never seen the likes of before. They all knew that the money in the photo is real money. It isn't hard for them to figure out at that point that the man standing before them was the real deal.

A hand goes up.

"Yes, sir?" Donnell asks the young man.

"Man," Mr. White, "you had all that bread..." *Bread meaning money.* "Why you didn't quit while you were ahead of the game?"

A few others chimed in uttering "Yeah, for real though, you were crazy," Mr. White.

"Well, that's an easy one to answer for you guys. Honestly, I think you may already have the answer to that question. It exists within the reality of your current situation. This might sound like a stupid question to ask but have you ever committed any crimes in your lifetime?" Mr. White asks the young man.

"Ummm, duh," Mr. White... "Why else would I be behind bars?"

"Alright, how many times did you commit those crimes before being caught?"

"I really can't say," Mr. White, "because I was on the streets for a minute now before I got caught."

"But you kept committing those crimes until you eventually got caught. Right?"

"I guess so... Yeah, you can say that."

"Did you ever think about stopping while you were ahead?"

"Not really."

"Why not?"

"Probably because I was way too busy getting money to be thinking about getting caught or anything else for that matter."

"Precisely my point. I rest my case. The more we get away with things, the more we tend to have a false sense of *Invisibility.* We've seen it in the movies and in real life. Gangsters hardly ever decide to retire. Normally they're forced into it. The signs are there all along and so are the consequences thereof. Somehow the illusion of escaping karma trumps all logic. We then exercise rationality over common sense and see no reason to stop. I hope that this answered your question."

The expression on the faces of the boys and staff said it all.

Boy, were they all discombobulated.

From that moment on they all knew that they had to thoroughly think their thoughts through before presenting them to Mr. White.

Chapter 20
Memory Lane

"If it's ok with you fellas, I'd like to pick up where I left off when I first met you guys that day in the courtroom. At age 12, I had no clue that the choices I'd made would affect my life forever.

I had a 17-year-old cousin named Tye, who was known to most as Big Tye. He was 6ft. 5inches and weighed over 300lbs. He was a high school senior that played defensive end on the football team and he was extremely popular. To this day, I still haven't figured out why he let me hang out with him given the huge age gap between us. Tye had a candy coated painted brown 1988 Chevrolet Impala with chrome wheels and he had a sound system to be envious of.

I remember us driving along the 10-mile strip of roadway at Pensacola Beach during the summer. The best day to hang out on the beach was Sunday. Sundays on the beach were a sight to see and the place to be at back then. It was a time and place where thousands of people, young and old, gathered to barbeque, hang out, and showcase their cars. Hundreds, maybe thousands, of people were lined up on both sides of that 10-mile strip. Cops patrolled the area by helicopter, bicycles, and in their cruisers. All the girls wore

The Compass of a Conscience

shorts showing next to nothing or a combination of shorts and bikini tops. Cars, street bikes and motorcycles were on display all over the place.

The girls hung around the cars and bikes they liked, hoping to get a photo next to or on one of them. And whenever they took a picture with us in my cousin's car, "I felt like a superstar!"

There was no kind of jealousy or hatred among the fellas either. If they liked how you rolled, they'd come up and give you some "DAP." *A Dap is an urban hand gesture or handshake symbolizing mutual respect between two parties on the streets.* Tye was well-respected and knew so many people that he got daps regardless of what he had or didn't have.

Around sunset was when the crowd would start to thin out and everybody headed elsewhere. Me and Tye, would leave the beach to go to the next spot where the crowd had already been forming. The later it got, we'd leave, and he'd take me home. I'd be hyped with excitement thinking I couldn't wait to do this again next weekend.

[The boys laugh and giggle then.]

This was our regular routine for the entire summer. One night while out with Tye, I was introduced to a couple of unsavory friends of his. As it turned out nothing about that night would be ordinary for me, I assure you of that. That night, I was caught up in the middle of a shootout.

Some guys tried to kill Tye's friends over a drug deal gone bad. It was revealed later that Tye's friends had sold these guys some fake cocaine for a lot of money. There I was, sitting in the backseat of Tye's car watching as Tye's friends passed this small plastic bag back and forth to each other.

Tye had stepped away for a second to entertain a female who had caught his attention. They were using a single car key to dip into the bag, place it under their nose and sniff. At first, it looked frightening, yet interesting at the same time. I had no idea that I'd be influenced into drug use in the form of peer pressure. In my opinion, they should've been car salesmen the way they sold me the idea of euphoria. Through their gyrating and analogies, they convinced me to give it a try. Tye came back just in the nick of time and stopped them from getting me hooked on cocaine. If not, maybe I'd be telling this story from the viewpoint of an ex-junkie and not an ex-dealer.

As his friend was about to pass me the baggie, Tye yelled, What the f--k you think you doing? He too young for that sh-t man. I better not ever catch you trying my little cousin like that again.

Moments later, a small Tan Mazda Rx7 zoomed in fast and two guys jump out. I could hear them yelling, Y'all sold us some fake sh-t and you n-@@as better straighten us right now.

One of Tye's friends responded, N-@@a, you know how the game go; somebody got us so we gotta pass it on to the next man.

The next thing I knew guns were drawn and bullets flew. I hit the floor scared as hell, as listened to the loud discharge of the guns piercing through the metal of Tye's car where I was trapped in. Once the shooting stopped all I could hear was girls screaming and car tires screeching off. I slowly but cautiously lifted myself up to get a view of what was happening.

Tye, as big as he was, lay low to the ground bear crawling his way to the door. He opened it and hopped behind the wheel, but before he started the engine he looked at me and asked, "You hit kinfolk?"

I was 12 and I wasn't quite familiar in understanding the dialect of the streets, so I had no clue of what that statement meant.

"I said, Huh?"

"Tye said, are you shot?"

"I said, Oh... No, I'm ok."

"Good. Just stay low while we burn out of here, said Tye."

That scared me even more, so I immediately dropped back to the floor hoping not to hear anymore gunshots. During the drive home that night my thoughts and emotions were all over the place. Something strange had begun happening within me. I went from being a cowardly kitten to becoming a "*Thundercat.*" I had this weird notion that I had cheated death and began bragging about the incident to all my friends.

From that moment on, I had my mind made up on what I wanted to do. No one was going to stop me. One would think that I would have been deterred from that kind of lifestyle given the experience I just had. But it didn't.

Let me tell you fellas something. The old saying that trouble is easy to get into but hard to get out of is so true. Trouble is something that you must never go looking for because it's already looking for you. That statement would eventually become the soundtrack of my life."

Chapter 21
Moving Too Fast

"Prior to reaching the level that I ended up making it to, I had years of trials and errors that helped me develop the maturity I needed to survive in the streets. As far back as I can remember, I've always been a thinker with a hustler's mentality. I was somewhere around the age of 11 when I started my first business believe it or not.

My definition of a business, whether it is correct or not, is: *Any entity that is for profit and has employees.* That description would be indicative of what I had indeed accomplished at that age.

I turned a chore that I absolutely hated into a profitable business venture. My mom would make me rake the yard, and because I abhorred it so much, I'd think of ways to escape doing it. As fate would have it, one day my mom interrupted my duties to send me to the store for flour. On the way to the store, there lived a man named Franky, who had the nicest home in our entire neighborhood. It was painted white with green trim and had a screened-in front porch. There was only one problem that everyone seemed to have with Franky's property. That problem was his rebel dog. It was a Great Dane that he had named Fuji.

Fuji was an aggressive dog. He would charge towards the gate barking at every passerby. There had been instances when Franky forgot to close his gate, and Fuji would run out onto the sidewalk at people. Having had this happen to me several times, I took with me the rake that I was using for protection against Fuji. That day Franky and some of his friends, who all had very nice cars parked outside, invited me in. At first, I was scared to open the gate because of Fuji, but then I was amazed over the amount of control Franky had over him. All he had to do was yell at him and that huge dog would walk away lowering his head.

I opened the gate and, as soon as I entered the screened area of the porch, the distinctive aroma of smoke hit my nostrils. In the right corner of the porch stood a huge black table, partially covered by a white tablecloth. It had dominoes on top of it. All of Franky's friends were gathered around it playing, cursing and, of course, smoking. He asked me where was I headed to, and I said, to the store for my momma. He then asked me what I was carrying that rake around for. Thinking that he already knew my intentions of whacking his dog upside the head, I immediately replied, Oh, nothing... No reason.

He said, Well, that's too bad because I was looking for a yard boy to rake this yard for $20.00." To a poor kid like myself, $20.00 was the equivalent of a hundred-dollar bill. I wasted no time recanting my statement and said, I wanted to rake his yard for the $20.00.

Franky looked me square in the eyes and said, If a man or anybody ask you about anything you may have or might be doing, be honest with them. You never know how they may be of help to you. Don't drop ya books boy because you just might lose your lessons.

"Ok," I replied.

Franky dismissed me and told me that I could get started on his yard after I was finished running the errand for my momma. I ran to the store and I ran back home so that I could get started on Franky's yard. It took me the rest of the day to finish it, but I was determined to earn that $20. Towards finishing and filling up my last trash bag, an elderly lady pulled up next to me asking me if I did yard work. This time, I was wise enough to know how to answer a question like that. One yard led to another and before I knew it, I was overwhelmed with work. So, I bought two more rakes and began to recruit my friends.

There I was, an 11-year-old running a business, helping my mom and employing my friends all at the same time. Franky took notice of how smart a kid I was, and he developed a special interest in me. Every chance he got he'd stop and ask me to hang out with him on his porch. We'd discuss many topics of life such as money and girls. Not once did it ever occur to me that Franky was grooming me for what he would introduce me to a year later. The experiences I had with my cousin Tye was child's play compared to what I'd eventually learn from Franky.

In the beginning Franky seemed interested in me doing his yardwork and getting my education. He'd always say: "*Youngsta, you are a born leader and you're way too advanced for the crowd I see you with.*" Things pretty much remained that way for the rest of that year.

I started hanging out with Tye and skipping school more frequently. The more I skipped school, the more I'd run into Franky somewhere. He would always say, "*I know what you're up to youngsta.*" Slowly, but surely, I started seeing another side of Franky.

Franky would take me to private locations and allow me to see everything that was going on. Not one time did he try to force anything on me. He was planting seeds in me that he knew would be very profitable to him soon. Franky's philosophy was to find, mold, and create a young soldier to carry out what he himself couldn't. Ironically, I became exactly what he was looking for.

A crash dummy!

Somehow, he knew that by introducing me to that lifestyle I'd eventually want in on the action. Franky's influence on my life caused me to grow up way too fast. The first time I received oral sex, it was from an adult female, compliments of Franky. She was so pretty that I got a little nervous, and I think she knew it. She told me not to look at her, and just to lay back. So, I did. Afterwards, she got up and walked out. I gathered myself together and followed her. When I came out into the hallway, she and Franky were whispering to one another. When he noticed me standing there, he walked towards me with a sinister-like grin on his face. He grabbed me by the shoulders and said, You ain't no virgin anymore now youngsta.

I was upset because I really looked up to Franky and wanted his approval. Not knowing what they had been discussing bothered me. I kept asking Franky what she had told him. Recognizing my insecurities about the situation, Franky told me exactly what I wanted to hear to feed my little ego. A bunch of encouraging lies! It was time for me to graduate I assume, because we went straight to Franky's house, and he showed me his stash of cocaine, crack, and marijuana. Franky spent weeks showing me the ropes and where the money spots were. Franky only had three simple rules that he insisted I learn before he could cut me loose.

1. Watch your surroundings and the people around you.

2. Whatever you do, be sure you do it by yourself.

3. Talk less and listen more.

Franky said if I stuck to those principles along with the intelligence I already had, that I'd be successful. Not only did I embody those principles, as Franky taught me, "I became them." I would live by them throughout the years as I sold dope. Franky was the one who taught me the game and he was the first person to put drugs into my hand. As I did before by recruiting my friends to help me rake yards, in like manner I did to help me sell Franky's drugs.

Unfortunately, that's my time for today fellas. But I will be back to see you guys soon."

Simultaneously, they all begin complaining. "Ah man, already? You were just getting into your story," Mr. White.

"I know, I know," Donnell says. "Oh, and, by the way, Brandon is doing just fine. I will visit him in the morning. Is there anything you guys would like for me to tell him?"

There was an outpour of *"Get-well"* wishes. Ranging from, *"Tell that boy we holding him down in here,"* to *"Tell him I said to stay up,"* to *"Keep his head on a swivel and his back against the wall,"* to *"Watch out for everything and everybody."* As strange as these *"Get-well"* requests may seem to some, Donnell understood what each of their statements meant.

Chapter 22
Heart to Heart

The next day, Donnell arrives to the hospital and enters Brandon's room. Brandon is distracted watching television and does not notice him standing there at first. Out of impulse, Brandon turns, and to his surprise, he sees Donnell standing there holding a bag. A peculiar look shows across his face. It was as if Brandon had seen a ghost or something. With teary eyes, he smiles and says, "Man," Mr. White, "where have you been?"

"I've had a lot going on," Brandon. How are they treating you in here?

"The hospital ain't that bad but... Brandon partially raises his arm displaying cuffs. "As you can see, I've had visitors."

"Oh wow. I see..." Donnell says. "When did this happen?"

"I don't know," Brandon says. "My guess would be last night as I slept because I woke up and these cuffs were on me this morning. As if I am going to walk out of here."

They both burst into laughter.

"Speaking about visitors," Mr. White, "some crazy sh-t happened yesterday."

"Oh yeah? What happened, Brandon?" Donnell asks.

"Two fake a-- wannabe Christians came in here talking about praying over me to speak in tongues."

"Tongues? Are you serious," Brandon?

"Hell yeah, I'm serious! IN TONGUES," Mr. White!!

"How well did that turn out for you," Brandon?

"Man," Mr. White, "I told them devil worshipping muthaf--kas to get the hell out of my room with all that f--kery. Well... not exactly in those words. So, I guess you know that they call themselves putting a curse on me, right?"

"Huh? How so," Brandon?

"I don't know," Mr. White. "Honestly, I really don't care. That's just what they said to me."

"Be careful with that stuff," Brandon. "Don't let strangers lay hands and pray over you."

"They didn't do anything to me period! That was their response after I went off on their a--es."

"Ok then," Brandon. "Let's change the subject to other things I think need to be discussed and dealt with."

"Like what," Mr. White?

The Compass of a Conscience

"Like your language for starters. You got to learn how to communicate what you are trying to say without so much vulgarity."

"Vulgarity? What the hell does that mean? Don't start tripping on me," Mr. White.

With a smile on his face, Donnell gently starts explaining to Brandon that vulgarity means the foul language he uses. "Another thing," Brandon? "How far did you get in school?"

"School? First, you come at me for being myself and speaking my mind. Now you trying to come at me like I'm stupid or something? Man, I don't know what you got up your sleeve but you're acting strange' for real," Mr. White.

"Brandon, calm down. I'm only asking these questions to understand you better. Unfortunately, you gotta do a thorough background check on people nowadays. You just never know who you're dealing with. I'm not referring anything to you either, Brandon. But, I'm interested in knowing everything about you. Your family, upbringing, education, etc... All are very important to me. In return, you get to know everything about me also."

"Mr. White, there are things that neither you nor anybody else need to know about me. That's real talk!"

"That's just it," Brandon! "God allowed our paths to cross for a reason. It is by his design that we are in each other's lives. Did you know that the best book ever to be read by you, will be written by you? You want to know why?"

"Not really," Mr. White. "But I have a feeling you're gonna tell me, right?"

"You betcha," Brandon. "It will be, because it will be illustrated with real life occurrences that you've survived. These experiences will be interpreted from a personal as well as a practical point of view. What I believe is that beneath that tough exterior you have going on for everyone is a very deep story. I'm talking about the kind of story that can help to change so many lives," Brandon.

"If only you knew," Mr. White, "just how messed up my life really is. You wouldn't feel the way you feel, trust me on that."

"You can't possibly think that your story is anymore jacked up than mine," Brandon. "I've done some foul stuff in my life. God continues to use my story to make a difference in the lives of others, including you."

"But there's a difference though," Mr. White.

"How so," Brandon?

"Because you haven't even heard my story to compare it to yours."

The Compass of a Conscience

"Ah- Ha! Do you realize what you just said to me," Brandon?

"What did I say," Mr. White?

"You've proven the point I've been trying to say all along to you. For us to completely understand one another, we must know each other's story. If you think about it, you know all about my past because I've told you about it. Trust me, Brandon. I'm not trying to get all in your business like that.

Try to remember that I'm from the streets too and you know that I know the rules. I believe that I have a right to know who I'm dealing with, and so do you. If we are going to be in each other's lives, then all cards must be on the table. Capeesh?"

"C'mon," Mr. White. "Enough with the big words already. I know that you're smart and all, but you gotta remember I'm from the streets too. You and I both know n-@@as from the street don't talk like that."

"Fair enough," Brandon. So, are you going to answer my question?

"What question? You've asked so many that I've lost track of them."

"School," Brandon. "When was the last time you attended a school? Please try not to think that you know what I'm thinking either. I just want to know."

"Honestly, it's been a long time," Mr. White.

"Oh, wow! Well, in this bag I have some educational literature that I'd—".

"Mr. White, it's been a while and I was a kid then. I'm not a kid anymore and I'm definitely not interested in school right now."

"Last I checked being a 16-year-old still qualifies you as a minor. So, technically you are a kid in the eyes of society. Look, Brandon, if you want to change and be a better person, you've got to be willing to elevate your mind first.

"I'm just curious," Brandon. What have I done to make you feel as though you can't trust me?

"Nothing. But I'm just saying though..."

"But nothing. You can't play the middle. It's either I have or haven't," Brandon, interjects Donnell.

"Alright, Alright, Ok! Let's see what you got in your bag there," Mr. White.

"I really appreciate you having an open mind about this, Brandon. It shows me your true character. Also, while we're at it, what's the story on your parents?"

The Compass of a Conscience

"What about them? I mean, what are you asking me about them for?"

"It's because I can't help but wonder how you ended up being a ward of the state. What bothers me even more is why aren't your parents by your side through all of this?"

"You know what" Mr. White? "I can't say if I remember anyone I've ever known ask me about my parents."

"Really? Are you kidding me," Brandon?

"No. I'm being so serious right now," Mr. White. "Believe it or not, I haven't talked to anyone about my parents because it's just better that way. But for some strange reason I have this weird feeling that you're like family to me. Somehow that makes me feel comfortable to talk about my parents with you."

"I'm honored that you feel that way about me," Brandon. "I can assure you that whatever we talk about will remain between God and the two of us. I'd like to hear what you have to share about your parents."

Chapter 23
Misplaced Anger

"Well, from what I can remember and from what I was told, my dad was a big-time cocaine dealer. He wasn't home a lot so there's not a whole lot to remember about him. The one thing I'll never forget was how cold hearted he was. And although I was barely old enough to remember, I still have the memories of how mean his a-- was.

I have this one memory that I can't get out of my head no matter how hard I try. It was of him roughing up my older brother DJ. Every time he would beat my mom up, DJ would jump in to protect her. I was a coward and just sat there crying as I looked on. DJ is a few years older than I am, so we were pretty close and did everything together."

"Oh, so you do have family then," right?

"Not really," Mr. White.

"Wait a minute... I'm confused. Didn't you just say you had a sibling named DJ?"

"Yes. I also have a younger brother named Jaylen, but we call him Jay Baby. Me and DJ was raised by our grandma and Jay is being raised by our aunt."

The Compass of a Conscience

"Ok, now I'm really confused. How do you have not only one but two siblings, and Child Protective Services not know any of this?"

"Oh, they know about it," Mr. White. "As a matter of fact, they know everything about me. I have a long and complicated story. You have no idea what I've been through and it will take a lifetime to tell you it all."

"Well, today must be my lucky day. I just so happen to be available to hear what you have to say."

"Talking about this isn't easy for me," Mr. White. If you talk about this to anybody, we'll never be cool again."

"Are you for real," Brandon? "You mean to tell me that we're still on that? So, I'm back to proving myself to you again, huh?"

"You don't have to prove yourself to me," Mr. White. "This is so deep, and I can't share this information about myself with just anybody. This affects more than just me. It affects my family as well."

Donnell looks at Brandon square in the eyes and says, "What we discuss will remain between us. I mean that," Brandon. "On the surface of things, I get the feeling that your parents may have messed up pretty bad to lose their kids."

"My parents are dead," Mr. White.

"Are you speaking of physical death or just an emotional death as far as you're concerned?"

"No," Mr. White. "They're really dead, like six feet under dead."

"Okay, I understand now. Do you mind if I ask how they died?"

"That's part of what I meant when I said my story is long and complicated," Mr. White.

"I have the time to listen but it's up to you if you feel comfortable talking about it," Brandon. "If not, I understand."

"I'm ok with us talking about it," Mr. White. "It's been years now and it doesn't bother me anymore. Basically, my dad was a very abusive man. I would say that I had to be around 8 or 9 years old at the time, but I'm not sure. What I am sure of is how old DJ was though. At that time, he just turned 11 and had his birthday party the day before everything went down.

The next day, my parents got into a fight. My dad punched my mom in the face and blood gushed from her nose. DJ ran into the bedroom and got daddy's gun. He walked up behind daddy and pulled the trigger repeatedly, but nothing came out. My guess is that the gun wasn't loaded, and DJ didn't know it.

The Compass of a Conscience

To this day, I believe that had that gun been loaded DJ would've killed daddy and my mom would still be alive today."

"That's a pretty harsh thing to say," Brandon. "Don't you think?"

"When you hear the rest of the story, you'll know why I feel this way," Mr. White.

"My daddy must have heard the clicks from the gun or something. He turned around to see DJ aiming the gun straight at him. He looked at DJ and said, What, you trying to shoot me, you little muthaf--ker? Sorry for cursing," Mr. White, "but that's how he said it."

"You don't have to explain yourself," Brandon. "This is your story not mine, and how you choose to express yourself is not for me to judge."

"Ok, so DJ starts crying because he's scared and don't know what daddy is about to do to him at this point. He drops the gun and runs into the laundry room locking the door. I personally thought daddy was gonna kill him but to my surprise he didn't. Matter of fact he didn't do anything but pick the gun up and leave. He did the strangest thing before he left though. As he picked the gun up and headed towards the door, he noticed me standing there watching. I swear to you it looked like he had a guilty look on his face.

For a few moments, he just stared at me before walking out the door."

"Wow! Where was your mom at during all of this?"

"She was in the bathroom trying to stop her nose from bleeding, I think. Daddy was gone by the time mom came out of the bathroom. I took one look at her face and all I could do was cry. He really messed her face up. She asked me what was wrong and why was I crying. I didn't say anything of course.

She asked me where my dad was. DJ and I told her what had happened between them. She got DJ and sat us both down and apologized for what had just happened. Mom loaded us into the car and we all went to the hospital. She cried the entire way there. The crazy thing is she didn't call the police on this dude. The hospital notified the authorities, but she made up a story to protect my dad from being arrested. The time we spent in the E.R. of that hospital seemed like an eternity and my dad was nowhere to be found. The hospital finally released momma and we went home. Little did I know that the next day would be the last time I'd see either of my parents alive again."

Chapter 24
The Robbery

"Things started out as like it usually did that day. DJ and I ate cereal for breakfast and rode our bikes around the neighborhood. We hung out at the park and over some friends' houses of ours until it was time to go home. When we got home it was time to take a bath and eat dinner. Momma was still cooking, so we sat on the couch in the living room and watched T.V. We could hear the loud pipes of our dad's motorcycle coming down the block. He pulled up and the single bright headlight briefly shined through the window before going off. Our dad walked in and the only thing he said was, "Where ya'll momma at?"

Too scared to say anything we both remained silent. He walked passed us and went down the hall to his and mom's bedroom. Mom was putting Jaylen to sleep on the opposite side of the hallway across from our room. About 30 minutes later a loud bang and a series of doorbell rings followed nonstop. DJ hopped off the couch to go answer and see who it was knocking the door. But before his feet could hit the floor, dad was in there. He told DJ to sit his a-- back down cause ain't nobody knocking for him. DJ immediately jumped back on the couch with me. As soon as he unlocked the door, it swung open hitting him in the face and knocking him to the floor. Several men came running in.

They were dressed all in black and wore ski masks. All we could see was them waving their guns at us. One of them pulled DJ from the couch onto the floor where they were already pistol-whipping daddy. They kept repeating, "N-@@a! You know what time it is. Give it up, n-@@a!" Two of them went to Jaylen's room. They dragged momma out by her hair to the living room where we were. By this time, my dad was barely recognizable because he had been beaten up so badly.

Seeing them handle momma so roughly wasn't that shocking to DJ and me. We'd seen our dad do worse things than that to her. This time was different because the circumstances were different. These were strangers whose identities were concealed underneath their ski masks. Daddy knew who one of them was because I heard him saying, "Fresh! This is where I lay my head, n-@@a! You gon do me in front of my family?" The guy started hitting my dad with the handle of his gun. He gave my dad a lick for every word. "DIDN'T-I-SAY-SHUT-THE-F—K-UP-N-@@A?"

After doing their sweep of our house, I was surprised that they didn't take Jay from his crib. Beating daddy didn't seem to be getting them anywhere so they decided to raise the stakes. One of them went outside and came back in with a gas can. They poured gasoline in a circle around us and said,

The Compass of a Conscience

"Give it up n-@@a! We ain't playin around no more." My mom said, "Why are ya'll doing this? These are our kids and they have nothing to do with what he got going on." The guy who I guess was in charge said, "B--ch! Who you think you talking to?"

He grabbed her by the throat and walked her back down the hallway into her and dad's bedroom. I could hear momma pleading for her life and ours too. This cold-hearted a—n-@@a wasn't trying to hear none of that. Mom said, "Please, I'm so sorry. I got kids and they're gonna need me."

The guy yelled, "Shut up, b--ch!"

I heard a loud thud and things got quiet in her room for some time. He opened the door and called one of the other dudes for help. Together they dragged my mom into the living room with us. Without a second thought, they dropped her face first on the floor in front of us.

Thinking that she was dead, I completely lost it. I jumped off the couch crying, "Momma! Momma... you ok, momma?"

I overheard the guy telling my dad, "I done f--ked over yo b--ch." He pulled a quarter from his pockets and said he was going to flip it. He wanted to act out some sort of twisted game of roulette in a very foul way. He said, "If this quarter lands on tails, I'm gone shoot you in the a--, n-@@a! If it lands on heads, I'm gone blow yo f--kin head off!"

The quarter must have landed on tails because at that point blank he shot my dad in the leg. My ears were ringing and hurting so badly. Jay had to have been scared by the blast too because by now he was crying. The guy told my dad, this is my last time telling you to give it up nigga! I'm about to f--k over these little f--kers next. Daddy stared at us for a few seconds and with tears in his eyes said, "Sorry, and that he loves us."

For long as I'd been alive, I'd never heard him say anything like that to us. He looked at the guys and said, Alright man, I ain't gon let you kill me in front of my kids. Take me to my spot, n-@@a, and you can have that sh-t."

Two of them picked momma up and daddy said, "She ain't going with us."

The guy in charge said, "What the f—k do I look like? I'm stupid or something? She definitely gots to go with us."

They walked me and DJ to the bedroom and the dude told us if we were smart, we'd stay our little a--es in that room. Two more shots rang out and we heard the door slam and the burn of car tires. All this time Jaylen had been crying his little lungs out and all we could do was sit in silence. We stayed put in that room for at least two hours and Jaylen had been crying the whole time. DJ went in the room and got him and brought him back into the room where we were. He said, "come on, let's go. But I was too scared to move. That's when he yelled at me "ain't nobody in there anymore. They're all gone. Come on," Brandon!

"I got up and we left quickly. We stayed at the end of a dead-end street. Our house was deep in the cut so there was very little light around it. Our aunt and uncle stayed a few blocks over, but it didn't seem like it that night. Every time we saw headlights or vehicles approaching, we'd run and hide thinking it was the robbers coming back to kill us. We finally made it to our aunt's house and she must've called every agency of law enforcement there was. That pretty much led to her getting custody of Jaylen."

"Eventually they caught the robbers and charged them with capital murder for the death of our parents. The cold part of it all is that the courts couldn't convict them of capital murder because my parents' bodies were never found.

I'm stuck with the memories and I can't get rid of them no matter how hard I try. Honestly, Mr. White, I get what happened to my dad because of the lifestyle he lived. What I'll never understand or accept is why my momma had to get caught up in his sh-t, man. Every time I think about what happened to her, I get so mad at God just thinking about it. If He loved us so much like the preachers say that He do, why would He let something like this happen to someone who was as sweet as my momma? The police stopped searching for their bodies and no one knows nothing or seem to care so

I stopped caring. I stopped caring about God, my family, or myself... I stopped caring about life."

After speaking those words things got very quiet in that hospital room between Donnell and Brandon. They both stared at other objects in the room but what they had just talked about dominates their thoughts. It really does a number on Donnell and gives him a totally different perspective of Brandon. He feels useless to help Brandon cope with the loss of his parents. His heart is torn for this kid who has gone through so much. Over the next few weeks things begin to change in unbelievable ways in both of their lives.

Brandon allows Donnell to help him regain his interest in education. What is even more shocking is that Brandon slowly begins scaling back on using profanity. On the other hand, Mr. White scores a few victories of his own also. He and Ms. Oukinuwin begin dating and together they form The Boys Will Be Boys Foundation (TBWBBF), a non-profit organization that mentors and assists at-risk youths in reentering society upon release. The number of participants grows from a faithful few to over 50 youths in less than 90 days. The sudden increase of teenagers enrolling in the program doesn't affect Donnell's commitment to Ohallowbee or to Brandon. He continues mentoring at Ohallowbee and remains committed to supporting Brandon with education and physical therapy while he is in recovery.

Chapter 25
Time to Go

Donnell and Ms. Oukinuwin are out and about when Donnell's phone rings. On the other end is a frantic Brandon yelling hysterically.

"Man, they trying to get me and take me somewhere," Mr. White!

"O.K., O.K., calm down, Brandon," Donnell says. "Who and w-w-what is trying to do what to you, Brandon? I'm on my way there," Brandon. 'Just be cool until I get there," he tells Brandon before hanging up the phone.

Upon arriving to the hospital and exiting the elevator on Brandon's floor, Donnell and Ms. Oukinuwin run smack dab into the commotion coming from Brandon's room. As they enter the room the scene is somewhat disturbing. Brandon is surrounded by hospital officials and members of Ohallowbee's staff.

Mr. Jones has been called out because Brandon has a knife and refuses to allow anyone near him. Mr. Jones is the only person that has the authority to use force, if needed, to subdue Brandon. He intercepts Donnell and Ms. Oukinuwin and requests a private moment to talk to them.

Mr. White and Ms. Oukinuwin comply with Mr. Jones request, and he steps out of the room.

Mr. Jones explains to Donnell that the State can no longer afford Brandon's massive health expenses, and tells him that Brandon will be placed in the infirmary at Ohallowbee for the rest of his sentence. Mr. Jones, looking for an alternative to using force, asks Donnell if he can calm Brandon down. Also, if he could break the news to Brandon in a way that he could accept.

Concerned about Brandon's safety, Donnell readily agrees. He goes back into the room and speaks directly to Brandon. He explains everything to Brandon, and assures Brandon that he'll be in his corner no matter where he goes. Without any hesitation Brandon surrenders the knife and cooperates. True to his word, Donnell, along with the assistance of Ms. Eaton and Ms. Oukinuwin, secures an unheard-of visitation agreement with Mr. Jones.

The transport from the hospital to Ohallowbee's infirmary is very difficult for Brandon to adjust to at first. Mr. White's first visit is the only concern he has. Knowing that Mr. White is a man of his word is the only thing that brings any comfort to Brandon's mind. True to his word Mr. White shows up with a rectangular shaped box in his hands.

"What is that you've brought up here," Mr. White? Brandon asked upon seeing Donnell with a *Connect Four* board game.

"If you have an open mind," Brandon, "you might find a few comparisons to life hidden within the scope of this game."

"Oh boy! Here we go again. I ain't interested in playing no old board games," Mr. White.

"Just play a few games with me," Brandon, ok?

"Okay," Mr. White, "but I gotta say that you fooled me."

"How so," Brandon? Donnell asks."

"I was under the impression that you were a serious dude, but you come in here bringing games and stuff... I'm not so sure about you right now," Mr. White.

"It all depends on how you look at it," Brandon, Donnell says. "Don't be so quick to judge me or my intentions," Brandon. "Yes, I know it seems like certain things I'm doing make no sense to you. But what I am trying to bestow upon you can be complicated to understand at first glance. This kind of knowledge goes far beyond what you've seen and experienced in your life."

Donnell and Brandon play a few games, until Brandon gets frustrated. He throws up his hands in the air saying, "This is what I'm talking about, Mr. White! Every time I try to build a pattern, you block it, and nobody wins. Who would be stupid enough to invent a game where nobody wins?"

"I was hoping you would ask me something like that," Brandon. "By now you should know me well enough to know that I do things for a reason, right?"

"Mr. White, I never said I gave up. I just said this was stupid and I was tired of playing it."

"I never said that you said anything now," did I Brandon? "However, there is a lesson that needs to be taught here and I'd like to shed some light on it for you. Earlier in our conversation, I asked you to have an open mind. The reason why was because I felt like this game can be related to real life issues. The rules of life are simple, but they can also be complicated. Likewise, so are the rules to this game."

To succeed in both, the goal is to have things aligned in a row or in a certain order. The problem is, there will be those who will oppose you and complicate things for you. You see these slots and columns on each side of them? Let's just say that the slots are life's pitfalls and the columns are the walls we run into throughout our journey. I noticed that you used

The Compass of a Conscience

the same patterns as we played the game each time. Chances are, you've repeated the same behavior in your life thus far."

"I was just doing something because you insisted on me playing," Mr. White. "I wasn't trying to win or nothing like that."

"Allow me to finish before you get defensive on me," Brandon. "We all follow patterns in our lives. Whether it be religious beliefs or something as simple as the laundry detergent, we have a pattern. Patterns are nothing more than our "Ways," Brandon.

"Let's take an inventory of everything. You have slots/columns meaning -pitfalls and walls of life-; also, patterns -your ways- and then you got opposition -something or someone trying to prevent you from reaching your goals in life-. The objective of the game is the same one as life. You must get your ducks in a row while facing all these things. It's what I choose to call Design or Purpose, Brandon. Design is what you choose to make it. Remember I mentioned that your patterns or ways were the same each game we played?"

"Yeah, I remember," Mr. White.

"Well, it's not until you change your ways that you can see your Design or Purpose in life. Now, was that too deep for you Brandon?

"Actually, it was very interesting to hear you make so much sense from a frickin' board game. I know that it was your way of helping me take a long hard look at my life and how I've been living it. Pretty cool way of doing it too," Mr. White.

"Thanks," Brandon. "I appreciate you listening and I'm even more delighted that you understood the message."

Mr. White and Brandon are cracking jokes and having a few laughs when Officer Williams walks in. Almost immediately their moods change. Brandon's mood is entirely more severe than Donnell's as he gives Officer Williams a deathly stare.

Donnell notices the look on Brandon's face and wonders why Brandon is looking so serious. Officer Williams greets Donnell with a hello and walks to the other side of Brandon's bed. He leans over to check Brandon's cuffs momentarily. While he is distracted, Brandon uses his other hand to grab a fork nearby on his food tray. Donnell, seeing Brandon's intentions and knowing that scenario all too well, grabs Brandon's hand and removes the fork from his hand discreetly.

Brandon is a bit hesitant at first, but relinquishes the fork after Donnell stares him square in the eyes. Officer Williams finishes checking Brandon's cuffs and exits the room in the same fashion as he entered it. Mr. White wastes no time getting to the bottom of what caused that reaction from Brandon.

"The one thing that the streets have taught me was to never interfere with anybody's business Brandon."

"This ain't the streets, so tell me what that was all about Brandon?"

"Man," Mr. White, "there's a lot of stuff you don't know about and will not understand."

"Try me," Brandon. "See if I understand what you think I don't. Whatever it is, I know that he did something to you. You can tell me now or I'll find out later, but I will find out one way or another."

"He the reason I'm f--ked up like I am," Mr. White"

"Huh? What do you mean," Brandon? "I mean, how so?"

"All of us knows that he gay and be trying see who he thinks is weak, so he can... You know what I'm saying, Mr. White. His favorite thing to say is it's my word against your word.

You're a convict and I'm an officer. Whose word do you think they'll believe? He feels like he's *"Mr. Untouchable"* around there," Mr. White.

"Wow Brandon! That's crazy! That's exactly how he spoke to me when we had some words about what happened to you."

"You mean to tell me that you guys got into it," Mr. White? "How did that happen?"

"He had some harsh comments concerning your situation that I didn't take well at all. So, I let him have it."

"Between us two," Mr. White, "Officer Williams is the reason all this happened to me."

"How is he responsible Brandon?"

"This is what happened that night," Mr. White." It was around lights outs and a few of us got our showers cut short. As we normally do, we'd finish drying off and putting our lotion on at our bunks. When Officer Williams is on duty we all know better, so we don't do it, but my shower had got cut short. We all started rapping and freestyling against each other in a circle around my bunk. Everybody was enjoying themselves until Officer Williams burst in on us."

"Like roaches do when the lights come on, they all scattered except me because I already was sitting on my bunk. I tried to play it off like I was putting lotion on my feet when Officer Williams asked why I was out of uniform. I said, what are you talking about?

I don't have to be in my jumpsuit during lights out. He said, No, you don't. But all you have on is your boxers. Where's your shirt?"

"Before I could make up a lie or an excuse, he said some foul sh-t to me that set me off."

"What did he say to you," Brandon?

"He asked me why was everybody around my bunk? I must be giving them some... well, you know," Mr. White. "I ain't gonna repeat it because it doesn't sound right coming from my lips."

"So, what did you do," Brandon?

"I went "Ham" –*crazy*– on him, and somehow he ended up on my back choking me, till I passed out. The last thing I can remember was all the fellas jumping in before I lost consciousness. "You saved his punk a-- this time but you won't always be around to stop me. If it's the last thing that I do, I'm gonna kill him and that's on everything I love."

"Do you realize what your current situation is, and how you got here," Brandon? "Consider this for a second. If he could do this to you with the use of your legs. Can you imagine what he could do to you now," Brandon? "You're right. It is a good thing that I was here to save you and prevent him from potentially hurting you worse. Don't be stupid," Brandon. "You've got to start making better choices for yourself. Life is not a joke or a game to be played with."

"If you don't find a reason to live, don't worry. You won't live very long. I'm giving it to you 100% raw because you need to wake up for real. Obviously, God allowed this to happen to you for a reason. He needed to slow you down to get your attention. I believe God has plans for you, but you got to change your outlook on life, or it will destroy you. I will talk with Mr. Jones and have him meet me up here, so you can tell him what happened to you."

"Are you crazy," Mr. White, Brandon replies. "I ain't no snitch!! Don't come at me like I'm one either because I don't get down like that. I thought you were real Mr. White. If I had known you'd act like this, I would've never opened my mouth to you."

"You know," Brandon? Donnell says, "that proves what I've been trying to tell you all along, about the way you think. It took me some time to figure out that my mind would take me much further in life than my fists would. I see you haven't learned that lesson yet, but keep on living. It'll all come together for you one day. Telling the truth is not snitching. The truth is the truth! In your case, it will be exposing a very dangerous man, Brandon. He's harming kids that are completely defenseless from this kind of abuse. I guarantee you that you're not the first kid he's hurt, but you can be the last one if you act now. Consider this," Brandon.

"Officer Williams has been a correctional officer for all these years, and there's no telling how many kids lives he has ruined. Look at the situation he's put you in," Brandon. "There are countless other victims, I'm sure, that felt just like you do. You guys have allowed this man to continue his reign of terror for far too long. When will it stop," Brandon? "It's gotten late and I gotta get home now, but as you know, I will be back to see you. You mind if I ask you a question," Brandon?

"No. What's on your mind," Mr. White? Brandon asks.

"I'd like for us to pray before I leave," Donnell says.

"No problem," Brandon exclaims.

"Thank you, Brandon," Donnell says. "Ok, close your eyes and bow your head. If you like to you can repeat after me openly or within yourself. Either way, God hears you."

Donnell begins to pray.

"Dear Heavenly Father, it is in the name of Jesus Christ that we pray. Lord, we come before your throne seeking by faith what we know that only you can do. Father, we know that you are the ultimate healer causing the blind to see and the lame to walk. We come boldly asking by faith that this young man be healed and we know that Brandon will walk again."

In the middle of Donnell's prayer, Brandon opens an eye and he opens his other eye seconds later. He zeroes in on Donnell's lips as if he wants to memorize the words that he is speaking. Suddenly, a tear forms in Brandon's eye and before he knows it, he is crying. Donnell, familiar with that kind of emotion during prayer, isn't fazed by it at all and keeps on praying.

After he's done, Donnell bids Brandon farewell. But there is something about Mr. White's prayer that resonates within Brandon's soul. Later, while lying alone in bed, Brandon decides to talk to God and say a prayer on his own. As best as he can remember Mr. White's words, Brandon is only able to get a straight sentence completed. Out of frustration, he blurts out loudly, *"God, if you are as real as everybody say you are, Let Me Walk Again!"* Brandon sobs to the point of exhaustion and falls fast asleep.

Around 5:15am, Brandon is awakened by an excruciating pain in his feet. And the more he rubs them it seems, the worse the pain gets. He plunges backwards into his pillow not knowing what to do. Suddenly, reality sets in and he realizes that he can feel pain now. Laying there he looks up at the ceiling and says, *"God, I know you're real now."*

Chapter 26
The Good News

"Hey, hey, hey! Tighten my line up or none of you will be going out for REC – recreation – today. You guys know what I require already. I'm tired of repeating myself to a bunch of morons who can't seem to follow simple instructions," Officer Williams says, belittling the group of detainees at the Ohallowbee Detention Center. "Keep this up, and I'm cancelling everything; including Mr. White's session scheduled for tonight because you will all be on lockdown. Now keep my line straight until the last person is in the hallway."

Officer Williams inspects his line and orders the group down the hallway into the day room. As they walk down the hallway, the boys and Officer Williams pass Mr. Jones office. Mr. Jones asked Officer Williams to step into his office for a minute. Nervous, Officer Williams wonders if Mr. Jones overheard him berating the detainees.

"Yes sir," Officer Williams replies to Mr. Jones.

Mr. Jones asks Officer Williams to close the door behind him. Once the door is shut, Mr. Jones pulls out a brown envelope asking Officer Williams if he knows what is inside.

Nervous, Officer Williams gulps and says, "N—no, sir. I don't."

Mr. Jones says, "This so happens to be a letter from the Mayor's Office commemorating a one Mr. Bernard Williams. It states, *Thank you for 35 years of dedicated service to the City of Pensacola and to the youths of its communities.*"

Mr. Jones stands up from his chair to shake Officer Williams hand, and adds: "This letter is from the Mayor himself. Why are you standing there looking like a bump on a log? You've done an outstanding job. Aren't you excited to receive this kind of recognition for all your hard labor?"

It takes Officer Williams a few seconds to process it all because at first, he thought he was about to hear some bad news. Officer Williams says, "Why yeah! I am more than excited to receive such an honor. I'm just overwhelmed, and I-I-I don't have words to express how I feel, so I'll just say thanks!"

Mr. Jones says enthusiastically, "Well, get out my office and go call your wife and kids to tell them the good news. Mr. White hasn't arrived yet, so you have time to talk to your family. I'm sure they will be so proud of you."

"Ok, thank you Mr. Jones," a relieved Officer Williams says.

"No, son. Thank you for your dedicated service to the boys here at Ohallowbee, and your commitment to this community." Just then, Officer Williams turns the doorknob to open the door and leave Mr. Jones office when all the employees of the Ohallowbee Detention Center are standing right in front of him, yelling "CONGRATULATIONS!"

Everybody greets him with congratulatory hugs and handshakes. There are drinks and snacks prepared for the celebration on long rectangular tables in the day room where the boys are. Everyone seems to be in a festive mood except the detainees. If expressions could talk, one could only imagine how much profanity would come out.

Donnell arrives about 25 minutes later unaware of the celebration going on inside the institution. As he makes his way through a security check, he proceeds to the day room where he is greeted by a very cheerful Ms. Eaton. She gives him a warm hug and fills him in on the reason for the celebration. Mr. White is furious about the news and asks Ms. Eaton to be excused. He goes to his car to blow off some steam and gather himself together to speak to the group. Thoughts of airing Officer Williams' dirty laundry surface, but Mr. White knows that this is not the place nor the time.

He re-enters the facility as the festivities are winding down, but Brandon's situation is all he can think about. Donnell asks the group if they are cool with it if he cancelled their session to go to the infirmary and visit Brandon. They all agree sending their *get well soon* wishes.

Chapter 27
It's A Miracle

The following day, Mr. White shows up to visit Brandon and receives the shock of his life. There is a physical therapist standing at the foot of Brandon's bed instructing him to lift his legs and wiggle his toes. Donnell stands there in total disbelief watching Brandon carefully lift his legs and wiggle his toes.

Just when the tears begin to form in his eyes, Donnell closes them to silently give thanks to God. He decides not to distract Brandon while he's in therapy and turns to leave.

He doesn't get very far before hearing a familiar voice calling, "Mr. White!"

The voice he hears has a distinctive tone of joy and happiness invoked by love.

"You see this?" Brandon tells Donnell as he raises his legs one at a time.

"Bran-Bran, you're the man! I see it!!" Donnell says, as he begins to stutter. "What... I mean, how... Well, when did all this happen," Brandon?

"Do you remember when we prayed the other night," Mr. White?"

"Yeah," Donnell replies.

"Well, after you left, I couldn't sleep. So I started praying. Then I fell asleep. The next morning it happened and now I know that God is real. No one can tell me different now," Mr. White.

"God is still in the miracle business," Brandon, Donnell says. "You are living proof of what his power can do. Now, we got to pray that God helps you stop cursing so much," Brandon.

[They both have a laugh.]

"On another note, I'm not sure if it's a good time or even if I should be mentioning this to you at all. I don't want to put a damper on all this good news that I'm hearing," Donnell said.

"What's on ya mind," Mr. White? Brandon asks. "You know that we're not supposed to be keeping secrets from each other remember? Nothing can spoil my happiness right now, I can promise you that."

Donnell looks at Brandon and then he looks at the physical therapist, who then excuses herself from the room.

"Ok, Brandon, here's the deal," Donnell says. "Yesterday I came up here for my regularly scheduled session with the group only to find out that there was a party being thrown in Officer Williams' honor. Apparently, the Mayor's office is giving him recognition. But wait till you hear why he's being honored," Brandon.

"He is getting a service award for his outstanding work with At-Risk youths in the community. If that's not enough to give you an upset stomach, there's more. They are really going all out for this creep. He will be featured on the front page of the newspaper and they're planning this huge ceremony in his honor at City Hall. What's worse than that is the guest list. It consists of some very prominent and influential people that have confirmed to be in attendance for this fiasco."

"Excuse my language," Brandon, "but this really pisses me off! They are literally creating a monster without knowing it. The thought of this worm possibly being catapulted into a higher position of power to continue abusing kids really bothers me, that's all."

As Donnell continues rambling on about the situation, Brandon begins to evaluate a few scenarios in his mind. While doing so, Donnell interrupts him by asking, "Brandon, are you listening to me?"

"Uh huh, I hear you, Mr. White," Brandon says.

"I have to get going now," Brandon. "I have a few things to get done today," says Donnell.

"Long after Mr. White leaves the infirmary," Brandon wrestles with disturbing thoughts about Officer Williams.

Chapter 28
The Proposal

It's been several weeks now, and Brandon is making remarkable progress in rehab. He is placed in an area called Special Housing for inmates who are in recovery from serious injuries or other medical conditions. Brandon is now walking on his own. It is in Special Housing where Brandon begins to make the effort to become a better person not only in spirit but also in school. He enrolls into every educational curriculum offered by Ohallowbee and excels beyond everyone's expectations of him.

Donnell and Ms. Oukinuwin have gotten quite cozy romantically with one another, moving into a condo along the seashores of Pensacola Beach, Fl. With the assistance of Ms. Oukinuwin, Donnell is reaping the harvest of seeing his goals being established with the *"Boys Will Be Boys Foundation(BWBBF)."*

Things were a bit slow at first but are at full throttle now. Although he doesn't know it yet, Donnell has a vested interest in Brandon becoming the face of the *BWBBF.* Donnell pushes Brandon hard to complete assignments and read as often as he can. He gives Brandon the communication skills that he feels will be important for him to have down the line. The two of them have become so close that a father/son-like relationship has begun to form.

One night, while at the dinner table with Ms. Oukinuwin, Donnell slides his chair back, takes a knee in front of her and pops the question.

"Oleta Oukinuwin, most of my life has been incomplete. I'm a man of numbers so when things don't add up, I get confused. All these years of things not adding up in my life are summed up in the person of you! I want you to be the first paragraph of my life and complete the rest of the story with us. What I am asking you is will you marry me?"

Donnell opens a small red velvet box that has a 2karat diamond ring inside.

Sitting there, stunned, with tears streaming down her face, Oleta leans down forward and kisses Donnell passionately.

"Does that answer your question?" She asks him?

They both hug each other. Donnell places the engagement ring on Oleta's finger. Needless to say. What happened thereafter.

While lying in bed, Oleta and Donnell start talking about Brandon, and he shares a little about Brandon's plight with her. Then, he tells her about Brandon's whole ordeal with Officer Williams. Mr. White goes on to tell her about his desire to adopt Brandon, but he knows that given his past criminal record it's not even an option.

Oleta stares deeply into Donnell's eyes feeling the sincerity and passion of his soul, and informs him that there may be a way to file for adoption once they are married. Jokingly, Oleta adds, "Shoot, I just may have to dump you and adopt the kid myself." They start laughing and fall asleep in each other's arms.

Chapter 29
Instant Karma

The day for Officer Williams' ceremony at City Hall finally arrives. From the look of things, you'd think a big named celebrity was in town considering all the media coverage it got. The guest list consists of the who's who in County, City, and state politics. A red carpet greets community leaders as well as clergymen and interviews are being conducted all over the place. The entire staff of Ohallowbee and its detainees are present, except for Brandon. Strangely, and to everyone's dismay Mr. Jones, Officer Williams' boss is a no show for the event.

Meanwhile, a black limo arrives with the guest of honor and his family. They exit the limo to "applause and flashing cameras." Now, since the honoree has arrived, all in attendance make their way inside and take their seats. The Mayor is the Master of Ceremony and after a few congratulatory speeches are given, The Mayor announces that it is his distinct honor to introduce the man of the hour, Bernard Williams.

Officer Williams takes the podium and begins speaking. "Good evening friends, family, and colleagues. Working in this field wasn't my original choice, but somehow, some way, destiny has revealed itself to me. To be able to work with the At-Risk youth population has been so fulfilling. It's also a very rewarding experience to serve youngsters whom society has given up on.

If you give a child hope, they'll begin to believe; Whatever a child believes, they'll ultimately achieve; Once he or she has grown, they'll return the favor that was given to them- H.O.P. E. I've dedicated my life to helping these kids reach their true potential by giving them hope and I--"

While Officer Williams is speaking, he spots two sheriff deputies and his boss Mr. Jones standing behind the curtains at the end of the stage. He has a feeling in the pit of his stomach that something is wrong. One of the officers signals him to cut his speech short and he complies. He makes his way over to the end of the stage and as he is nearing it, he gets the shock of a lifetime. There it was staring him dead in the face. KARMA! Officer Williams is approaching seeing Brandon sitting in a wheel chair accompanied by Mr. White and Ms. Oukinuwin. The deputies ask, "Bernard Williams? Are you Bernard Williams," Sir?

"Yes," Sir. I am. What's the problem, officer?" Officer Williams asks.

"You are under arrest for aggravated battery of a minor, with the intent to kill."

Officer Williams looks back at his family seated in the front row. He drops his head in shame as he's escorted out in front of a stunned crowd. When asked how he got the courage to face and take down Officer Williams, Brandon says that he wanted to prevent Officer Williams from hurting more kids.

Because of Brandon's courage, other detainees came forward and talked about Officer Williams' abuse. Interviews were conducted by the Department of Juvenile Justice (DJJ) and the charges against Officer Williams began to pile up.

Brandon's release date is quickly approaching and as a ward of the state, he will have to return to a group home once he is released. Mr. White is worried about Brandon's living situation but Oleta, his fiancé, has a little surprise of her own. She researched Brandon's background looking for possible living relatives and discovered information on his older brother DJ.

DJ was a seaman in "The United States Navy." She had gotten in touch with him and found out that DJ had already taken guardianship of Brandon's younger brother Jaylen. DJ agrees to get guardianship of Brandon, and allows him to stay with Donnell and Ms. Oukinuwin. Brandon gets released and everything goes as planned for everyone. Under Donnell and Ms. Oukinuwin's roof, Brandon is enrolled into high school and is doing well academically. Brandon joins Donnell and Ms. Oukinuwin, mentoring for the *BWBBF* just as Donnell envisioned he would. At first the organization had mediocre success to attract At-Risk youths.

Brandon joins, and the number of participants enrolled was staggering. Overnight, it seemed like The Boys Will Be Boys Foundation had become the largest non-profit in Northwest Florida. Mr. White and Brandon's dynamic-duo motivational speaking routine is in high demand, garnering the attention of local hometown media. The media is in a frenzy over the huge impact that the Boys Will Be Boys Foundation is making. The two, Donnell and Brandon are featured in almost every publication there is throughout the city. Over the next 12 months both "father and son" have established a legacy in which they could build upon for time to come.

Chapter 30
Lies, Deceit, and Betrayal

A year has almost passed since Brandon's release and he has a birthday coming up. Brandon will be turning 17 years old and is asked continually about his college plans. On his birthday, Brandon and Donnell are scheduled to appear and speak to a group of young men. These young men are facing possibly being charged as adults on the federal level for the crimes they've committed. The group that's there is part of a federal initiative program for youth offenders.

When the time arrives, Brandon and Donnell head to the federal courthouse, where they had first met. Walking up the steps and into the building gives both Donnell and Brandon a moment of déjà vu. In their minds, they realize they were free men now, but had been prisoners themselves not long ago. Neither of them mentions to the other what they are thinking. They enter courtroom 401 where the Honorable Stacy Ransom is presiding.

Donnell and Brandon are seated after a brief introduction to the group. Brandon has this look on his face and Donnell can see that he's visibly disturbed about something. Donnell leans over and whispers, "What's wrong," Brandon? "Are you nervous?"

The Compass of a Conscience

"Not really," Brandon says. "It's just that I know one of those guys well. He is like a brother to me, and I haven't seen him in so long and I hate to see him caught up like this."

"Well, you already know that this is the big league and he's in some serious trouble now," right? Donnell asks.

"Yeah, I know." Brandon says.

Also attending is a gentleman called Arty Sumler. He is a journalist. He works for one of the most recognized magazines in the country and was invited to do a cover story on Judge Ransom. What he ended up getting was worth far more than what he'd expected. The judge walks in and allows Donnell and Brandon to start things off.

Arty Sumler and his cameraman begin recording as both Donnell and Brandon take turns telling and integrating their stories. They cover how they met, what they've been through together, and how the impact of The Boys Will Be Boys Foundation is changing lives in their community. It is almost an identical rehashing of the dramatic experience they both had witnessed before. Some of the boys let a few tears flow but the ones who didn't, asked sincere questions about how to change.

It is an awesome experience for Arty as he captures on camera a moment far beyond what he had bargained for. Arty decides to conduct an impromptu interview with Donnell and Brandon. He also asks them both if they would sign release forms allowing him to use the footage. They both sign and a few months later there is a four-page spread about them and the *BWBBF* in the nationally recognized magazine that Arty works for.

That publication literally catapults Donnell and Brandon into instant fame. Calls for interviews and appearances come pouring in from all over the country. It was as if everybody wanted a piece of this unusual duo. Riding on a wave like that, it wasn't long before the #1 rated T.V. show host Jonathan Jewish of the *"JJ in the Morning Show,"* wanted to have them as guests on his show.

Urged by his fiancée Oleta, Donnell hires a publicist to represent him and Brandon. The publicist goes straight to work on the on the *"JJ in the Morning Show"* appearance. Unaware of it, at the time, Donnell is oblivious to the change in Brandon's behavioral patterns. The old friend that Brandon had seen that day in the courtroom name was Earl.

Earl had contacted Brandon and the two of them had been spending time together. Brandon really had been trying to help Earl change, but it seemed Earl got the better of that exchange. Earl had mind control over Brandon, and used it to create enmity between Brandon and Donnell.

He'd tell Brandon things like, "You really don't know this man like you think you do," or "I believe that Mr. White is using you," Brandon.

The Compass of a Conscience

Brandon vehemently denied Earl's accusations at first but the jealousy of seeing Donnell and Oleta giving their attention to the boys in the program, caused Brandon to eventually succumb to Earl's ill-fated advice and slowly he began to slip back into his old ways.

The first thing to take a hit was his grades, as they plummeted to below average. Whenever Donnell got onto him about it, Brandon would bring up things that allegedly bothered him concerning Mr. White's relationship with others. One day, Ms. Oukinuwin found cigar wrap in Brandon's bedroom. To Donnell, that meant that Brandon was back in the streets but Oleta convinced him otherwise.

Out of fear that Brandon might be a hindrance to the BWBBF, Donnell sits Brandon down for a talk. He explains to Brandon that he is the poster boy and the face of the organization, also that there are kids who look up to and admire him. More to the point Donnell tells Brandon he can no longer participate in the *BWBBF* until he straightens up.

This only adds false validity to the lies Earl had been planting in Brandon's head already. Brandon is furious and discreetly moves out of Donnell and Oleta's condominium. Donnell searches for Brandon all night long in the streets to no avail, until he remembers that the streets don't talk.

After a couple of weeks of searching, Brandon calls and Donnell's ready to chew his head off. Thinking fast, Oleta, standing near her frustrated fiancé, tells him to calm down. Donnell speaks to Brandon, but he still isn't willing to come back home despite them having had an exceptionally good talk. Right after Donnell hangs up the phone with Brandon, he gets a call from their publicist. Donnell tells the Publicist everything that's unfolding between himself and Brandon. He tells the publicist that it is best to cancel the appearance.

The publicist informs Donnell that he doesn't believe that is a good idea and explains why. The publicist believes that Donnell should do it without Brandon, but Donnell disagrees. The publicist explains that the issue he's having with Brandon isn't what this appearance is about. He tells Donnell that the storyline of his and Brandon's movement is what this thing is about. The publicist breaks down the dynamics and purpose of the appearance, which he says is a cause that far exceeds either one of them. Donnell still isn't convinced that he should make the appearance, so he asks for a few days to think it over.

Days later, the publicist calls again and, on the other end, is none other than Jonathan Jewish himself.

"Hello, Mr. White. It's an honor to meet you, says Jonothan Jewish."

"Likewise, Mr. Jewish, Donnell replies."

The Compass of a Conscience

"Allow me to get straight to the point, Mr. White. I called you personally because I'd really like to have you on our show. Jonathan Jewish says."

"Mr. Jewish, I'm not sure if you have been informed of this but Brandon and I are not in a good place right now. I don't want to appear misleading on your show," Sir.

"I understand, Mr. White, Mr. Jewish says. I think that you should come on the show anyway, and if you're comfortable with it maybe we can get in a little discussion about your son?"

Mr. White asks Jonathan Jewish to give him a day or two to talk things over with his fiancée.

"No problem," Jonathan Jewish replies. "Not an issue Mr. White, go ahead and discuss it with your fiancée, I'll wait for your answer. Hopefully, it's a yes."

Mr. White and Ms.Oukinuwin have the discussion and he tells her that he wants to reject Jonathan Jewish's offer. Ms. Oukinuwin talks him out of it. She reminds him of his vision that he had when they first met. She also reminds him that although Brandon decisions in life may affect their image together, it has no bearing on God's purpose for their lives.

"Don't throw in the towel, she says, and abandon the rest of the boys who believe in you and need you in their lives."

Afterwards, Donnell calls his publicist to confirm his appearance, and a flight is booked for him.

The week of his departure is chaotic. He is featured on every local publication and doing interviews all over. By the time the date of his departure arrives, he is exhausted.

He and his fiancée Ms. Oukinuwin arrive in New York safe and sound and check into a very luxurious hotel reserved for them. The next day, they arrive at the *"JJ in the Morning Show"* studios and are led to the green room where they'll remain until show time.

They've never seen or experienced anything like this before. The producers, camera crew, makeup artists, everybody including Jonathan Jewish, come in and greet them. They even have a personal concierge service around attending to their needs. Quite naturally, Donnell is nervous, but having a microphone affixed to his tie, made him even more nervous than he already was.

The time is at hand and the show is set to start. Oleta is led out to a front row seat in the audience. The production coordinator places Donnell in a designated spot. There he must stay until he's signaled to come out. While standing there, he gets a text message from Brandon that reads *"I'm proud of you and I'm sorry."* The music plays, the signal is given, curtains open, and Donnell walks out to a standing ovation.

The Compass of a Conscience

He gets off to a great start with humorous responses to Jonothan's questions. All his jokes seem to go over well with the audience. That is, until Jonathan asks him to explain in detail what is going on with Brandon and what happened to cause things to go awry between them. Donnell struggles to find the right words to express himself but ends up crying instead. In true fashion as she's always done, Oleta abandons her seat, and takes the stage to comfort her fiancé. She hugs, cries and hold on to him saying.

"It's ok, baby. Take your time she says," as a stunned audience looks on in silence.

Ms. Oukinuwin whispers something into Mr. White's ear and he begins to lift his head. He opens his mouth, stammering a little before releasing a hard blow of "Whooh..." and Donnell proceeds to make an open plea to Brandon on live television. He goes on to say, "Brandon, I've given up on a lot of things and a lot of people in my life. I've had so many people turn their backs and give up on me as well, but GOD has taught me something that I will never forget," son. God taught me how to "LOVE."

Donnell looks at his fiancée Oleta and grabs her hand. "Brandon, *LOVE'S* got a face, *LOVE* has a voice, *LOVE* even has a body to express itself. We LOVE you and we will never give up on you, son. I may not know where you are right now, but you know where we are and how to reach us. Come home, son. We'll be waiting for you."

The mood throughout the audience is about as high as it can get on an emotional scale. Tears are flowing and the next thing you know, everyone is on their feet clapping and cheering for the couple. A member of the audience comes on stage to hug the couple, and protocol goes out the window. The audience lines up to hug and shake the couple's hand to show their support for them and Brandon. Ratings for the show soar, hitting an all-time high and surpassing the ratings of any guest that had ever been on the show before. Calls from viewers pour in asking for Donnell's contact info and about the *BWBBF*. From that moment on, Donnell, Ms. Oukinuwin, and even Brandon become the topic of much discussion nationally.

Donations and free professional services to aid the growth of the Boys Will Be Boys Foundation came in from all over. The couple returns home to a welcome befitting kings and queens. Once their plane lands and they make their way into the terminal, a large crowd holding signs greets them with thunderous sounds of cheering. It is unlike anything the couple has ever seen before.

Chapter 31
History Repeats Itself

Things are back to normal and, as he usually does, Donnell is volunteering his time at Ohallowbee's. As he addresses the boys, someone catches his attention. This is an unfamiliar face and Donnell knows all the boys by their names. He stops to introduce himself to the young man.

"Hi, I'm Mr. White. And you are?"

"Rodriguez," the young man, answers.

"Nice to meet you, Rodriguez," Donnell says. "If you stick around here for a while you and I will get to know each other on a first name basis."

Donnell continues with his session, speaking and encouraging the boys. Afterwards, Rodriguez asks Donnell if he has a moment to talk in private. Rodriguez says that he already knows who Mr. White is, and that he has something serious to tell him about Brandon.

Rodriguez tells Donnell who Earl is, and that he was a kid that Donnell had met before.

"Brandon and Earl are like brothers," Rodriguez exclaims. "It's like Earl has this hold on Brandon, and Brandon can't seem to tell him no to anything."

It all begins to make sense to Donnell now. No wonder Brandon wasn't himself that day in the courtroom, he thinks to himself.

"That's not what's important though," Mr. White, Rodriguez says. "Earl is about to set Brandon up to get offed! – murdered."

Mr. White's heart drops and he asks, "What do you mean? Why, if they're supposed to be like brothers?"

"On the cool Earl don't really see or respect that brother sh-t. Oops, my bad. I wasn't trying to curse," Mr. White, Rodriguez says.

"It's ok," Rodriguez, "you can be yourself around me. How is Earl planning on setting Brandon up to get murdered?" Donnell asks.

"Earl got a few Jack Boys -*robbers*- he kickin' it with and Brandon out there getting his hustle on real strong. Earl is snorting cocaine heavily and he's always needing Brandon to put him back on his feet every time he go broke. Brandon kinda snapped on Earl and told him that he ain't gonna be feeding his drug habit. I guess Earl felt some kind of way about it and told us that Brandon gotta go.

The Compass of a Conscience

"He thought I'd be down with that sh-t but that ain't me and besides lil' Brandon is alright with me, Rodriguez says. It's supposed to go down Friday at this trap house -Drug House– on DeVillers Street. Earl told Brandon that he got a major deal set up for him and that he needed him to bring at least 10 racks - 10k. I was gonna give lil' Brandon the heads up but as you can see, I got locked up. I'm telling you this because you're about the only person that can save lil' dude's life right now."

Donnell is stunned and thanks Rodriguez for giving him that information. On the way home, Donnell stops at a liquor store and buys a fifth of Hennessy. He's drinking and driving, thinking about Brandon. He knows that going to that trap house could place him in a life-threatening situation but decides Brandon is worth it.

Just when he makes up his mind to go, he gets a call from Oleta, his fiancée. Having a bad feeling that something is wrong, she pleads with him to come home and tell her what's bothering him. Hearing her cry on the phone proves to be more than Donnell could handle, so he goes home. He tells Oleta everything Rodriguez told him about Earl's plot to kill Brandon.

They both discuss the possibilities of what they can do to save Brandon's life. Oleta asks Donnell what he is planning to do. She reminds him of how much is riding on his shoulders, and that a lot of people are depending on him.

That night, Donnell doesn't get any sleep thinking about Brandon. It was as if he was reliving the experience that he had with his childhood friend Anton, all over again. He knows that he could never forgive himself if something bad happened to Brandon that he could've prevented, and prays fervently to God for an answer on how to get involved.

It's now 5am Friday morning, the day planned to kill Brandon. Donnell conducts a stake out of the trap house looking for Brandon. Hours have passed and its now noon, with yet no sign of Brandon. Oleta calls and she's stranded on the other side of town with a flat tire. Donnell leaves his post to go help her. While he's in route his phone rings and it is Brandon calling. Quickly, answering the call he is so relieved to hear Brandon's voice.

"I just wanted to check up on you," Mr. White, and hear your voice, Brandon says.

Donnell begs Brandon to meet with him and will not take no for an answer. Brandon reluctantly agrees but wants to meet at the trap house. Mr. White tells Brandon that's not a good idea, but Brandon insists on it or else Donnell can catch him on another day. Mr. White wastes no time agreeing with Brandon's demands. He reaches the location where Oleta is, and starts changing her tire. Donnell is almost done

The Compass of a Conscience

tightening the last lug nuts on her tire when Brandon calls again.

Brandon tells Donnell to hold off a few hours before he comes. Knowing what was about to go down, Donnell tells Oleta about it again. He tells her that he's got to try and get Brandon away from that house. She begs him not to go and tells him that he should call the authorities, but Donnell isn't listening this time. He speeds off heading back to the trap house. At this point, Oleta is a total wreck. She recently found out that she is pregnant but couldn't share the news with Donnell because of his mood and his concerns about Brandon.

Without thoroughly thinking things through, Oleta calls and informs the cops of a possible murder plot about to take place, which turns out to be a bad decision after all. Repeatedly, she calls Donnell's phone, but her calls keep going straight to his voicemail. Donnell has turned his phone off to avoid hearing her cry. He arrives to the trap house, runs up to the door and bangs on it until someone opens it. Brandon opens the door and, what a sight it is for Donnell to see that Brandon is alive. They go out on a wooden deck porch at the back of the house. Donnell tells Brandon everything about Earl setting him up. Brandon is furious with Donnell for accusing Earl of something like that and tells him he'd better leave. Donnell says, "If I'm lying to you," Brandon, "you don't ever have to speak to me again. Let's sit in my car and see who Earl shows up with."

Brandon decide to go along with it only so that he could prove Donnell wrong. Plus, he needed Donnell to leave so he could handle his business. Little did either of them know the cops and the robbers were on the way to their location. They enter the house and are leaving the house when three men in masks are approaching fast.

Relieved that Brandon is leaving with him, Donnell doesn't notice them. He tries to say something to Brandon but before he could say anything, Brandon yelled, "Watch Out, Mr. White!," and pushes Donnell to the ground.

Gunshots rang out and after the gunfire ceased, one robber is dead and the other two narrowly escapes being killed.

"Give me the gun," Brandon! Donnell yells.

Brandon hands him the gun and, just as Donnell walks over, and kneels down to unmask the robber, the cops arrive.

"Drop your weapon and step away from the victim, the cop orders."

Donnell complies with the officer's command, then is handcuffed and arrested. Being in the backseat of a police cruiser isn't anything new to Donnell. It wasn't like it was his first time, but at this point in his life, things were different. The stakes were much higher now and he had a lot to lose. As he sat handcuffed with reality setting in, Donnell begins to see his whole life flash before him.

He knows that this situation would be unlike anything he's ever faced before. The warning of his fiancé telling him that he should've let Brandon go silently haunts him. Nothing he's experienced in life prior to this moment wouldn't be enough to prepare him for what he was about to go through...

YOU CAN FIND THE REST OF THIS STORY IN THE COMPASS OF A CONSCIENCE PART. 2

AUTHOR'S REFLECTION

TO MY SON RAY....
May 22, 2017
How could I ever forget that day
A judge who didn't know me or you
Decided he'd take my son away
Life can be so unfair
I hope you read this poem one day
My proof to you to show I care
Written in love
TO MY SON RAY...
I don't blame your mom
Don't blame your dad
I don't blame anybody else
I tried to reason with selfish people
Instead of fighting for you myself
Life can be so unfair
I hope you read this poem one day
My proof to you to show I care
Written in love
TO MY SON RAY...
I often wonder how we both will act

When the two of us finally meet
Hopefully, you'll know the truth by then
So, with a hug we'll both greet
THEN....
LIFE WILL BE FAIR
I WILL NEED NO POEM THAT DAY
YOU'll GET TO SEE MUCH I CARE
HOW MUCH I LOVE YOU!!
MY SON RAY!!!!

I was inspired to write this as a token of love to my son. After a 2year court battle with his parents. Parental Rights that I never knew I had legally, were taken away from me because I didn't understand Family Law, or how it operates. I may have lost a battle but I'm still fighting the war.

My prayer is to one day be in my child's life, no matter how old he is. This poem will out-live me, that I'm sure of. It's forever recorded from the journal of my heart onto the pages of this book.

I'LL NEVER STOP FIGHTING FOR YOU SON!!!

The Compass of a Conscience

Love Your Father - Darnell D Wright

This photo was taken a month prior to the arrest that ultimately landed me in a federal prison. ($325,000usd). It was retrieved from my home by federal agents and put on full display in a courtroom for all to see. It was the first time that I was forced to look at myself, outside of myself. It continues to serve as a constant reminder then, and now that who you once were, doesn't have to be who you will become. I am a better person now and my past played a major role in it. This kind of success didn't last but the kind of success God has granted me to have now from legitimate business endeavors and hard work will last a lifetime. It's an amazing thing to see what God can do in a person's life. I should know... I'm living proof!

— **Darnell D Wright**

Made in the USA
Columbia, SC
28 December 2017